"I Came Back Because Of You, Hayden."

Because she'd never really forgotten him. "I can't move on. Not until I figure out what went wrong between us."

He looked at her with that electric gaze of his. "Hell, Shelby, that's an easy one."

"Please don't say it again. I wish I had the money to pay your father back."

He narrowed his eyes and walked toward her. "So what do you say to some sort of reparation? You give me what I paid for."

"What your father paid for," she said.

"I paid for it in ways you can never understand."

But she did and it made her ache to realize it. "A night of sex? Is that what you want? I don't think I'm worth a million dollars."

He stood within an inch of her now. "Not a night," he whispered. "How about a week?"

Dear Reader,

It's February and that means Cupid is ready to shoot his arrow into the hearts of the six couples in this month's Silhouette Desire novels. The first to get struck by love is Teagan Elliott, hero of Brenda Jackson's *Taking Care of Business,* book two of THE ELLIOTTS continuity. Teagan doesn't have romance on his mind when he meets a knock-out social worker…but when the sparks fly between them there's soon little else he can think of.

In *Tempt Me* by Caroline Cross, Cupid doesn't so much as shoot an arrow as tie this hero up in chains. How he got into this predicament…and how he gets himself out is a story not to be missed in this second MEN OF STEELE title. Revenge, not romance, plays a major role in our next two offerings. Kathie DeNosky's THE ILLEGITIMATE HEIRS trilogy continues with a hero hell-bent on making his position as his old flame's new boss a *Reunion of Revenge.* And in *His Wedding-Night Wager* by Katherine Garbera, the first of a new trilogy called WHAT HAPPENS IN VEGAS…, a jilted groom gets the chance to make his runaway bride pay.

Seven years is a long time for Cupid to do his job, but it looks like he might have finally struck a chord with the stranded couple forced to reexamine their past relationship, in Heidi Betts's *Seven-Year Seduction.* And rounding out the month is a special Valentine's Day delivery by author Emily McKay, who makes her Silhouette Desire debut with *Surrogate and Wife.*

Here's hoping romance strikes you this month as you devour these Silhouette Desire books as fast as a box of chocolate hearts!

Best,

Melissa Jeglinski

Melissa Jeglinski
Senior Editor
Silhouette Desire

Please address questions and book requests to:
Silhouette Reader Service
U.S.: 3010 Walden Ave., P.O. Box 1325, Buffalo, NY 14269
Canadian: P.O. Box 609, Fort Erie, Ont. L2A 5X3

KATHERINE GARBERA

His Wedding-Night Wager

Published by Silhouette Books
America's Publisher of Contemporary Romance

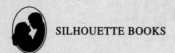 SILHOUETTE BOOKS

ISBN 0-373-76708-0

HIS WEDDING-NIGHT WAGER

Copyright © 2006 by Katherine Garbera

All rights reserved. Except for use in any review, the reproduction or utilization of this work in whole or in part in any form by any electronic, mechanical or other means, now known or hereafter invented, including xerography, photocopying and recording, or in any information storage or retrieval system, is forbidden without the written permission of the editorial office, Silhouette Books, 233 Broadway, New York, NY 10279 U.S.A.

All characters in this book have no existence outside the imagination of the author and have no relation whatsoever to anyone bearing the same name or names. They are not even distantly inspired by any individual known or unknown to the author, and all incidents are pure invention.

This edition published by arrangement with Harlequin Books S.A.

® and TM are trademarks of Harlequin Books S.A., used under license. Trademarks indicated with ® are registered in the United States Patent and Trademark Office, the Canadian Trade Marks Office and in other countries.

Visit Silhouette Books at www.eHarlequin.com

Printed in U.S.A.

KATHERINE GARBERA

One brief trip to Las Vegas and Katherine Garbera was hooked with endless story ideas and a fascination with that playground known as Sin City. She's written more than twenty books and has been nominated for *Romantic Times BOOKclub's* career achievement awards in Series Fantasy and Series Adventure. Katherine recently moved to the Dallas area where she lives with her husband and their two children. The only thing she loves more than writing is talking to readers. Visit Katherine on the Web at www.katherinegarbera.com.

This book is dedicated to Matt! Thanks for a fabulous wedding night and all the nights that have come after!

Acknowledgment

Special thanks to Chris Green who answered all of my Vegas questions and gave me an insider's perspective.

Thanks also to Natashya Wilson and Debbie Matteucci for their editing insight!

One

Long legs, expensive silk hose and the kind of hips that he could sink his fingers into. She had it all. She always had. Hayden still couldn't believe Shelby Anne Paxton was here in his kingdom. He'd never thought to see her again.

Her calves were well formed, tapering down to trim ankles and a pair of stilettos that sent his libido into overdrive.

The Chimera Hotel and Casino was his life. The 24/7 world of Vegas had always been his home. He wouldn't do anything to jeopardize the success of the hotel and casino. He'd sacrificed to make it into one of the premier destinations on the Vegas Strip. And he owed it all to this woman who hadn't believed in him and to his father.

Hayden had made the Chimera the number-one casino in Vegas to prove that their lack of faith wasn't an obstacle in getting what he wanted from life.

His entire operation was first-class, right down to the hotel's own shopping wing, which housed only sophisticated retailers. Always expanding and changing, it was about to add Bêcheur d'Or, a high-end lingerie boutique.

Bêcheur d'Or was on the fast track to the top. It's owners, Paige Williams and Shelby, had been profiled in *Entrepreneur* magazine earlier this year. Apparently Shelby had made more of his money than he'd ever expected her to.

But it had been Paige with whom he'd spoken to cinch the deal, and Paige with whom he'd met to sign the contract. Funny that Shelby had shown up here and now, especially considering he'd never expected her back in Vegas after she'd left him standing at the altar.

A long, low wolf whistle jolted Hayden back to the present and the hallway outside the newest merchandise location at the Chimera. "Well, well, well. What have we here?"

Hayden turned to see the tall, lean, dark-haired form of his best friend stroll up. Pain tightened in his gut. He didn't want even Deacon Prescott to know who this woman was. He'd simply referred to her as the gold digger that one time he'd gotten drunk and talked to Deacon about his marriage.

Hayden glanced at Deacon and fought the surge of possessiveness swamping him. "You're a married man."

"Definitely. But that doesn't mean I'm dead. Besides, Kylie knows I'd never stray."

Deacon and Kylie had been married for almost two years now and things were going well. They were the exception to Hayden's golden rule that marriage was a business deal.

"No, you wouldn't," Hayden said more to himself than to Deacon. Deacon had found something that Hayden would never admit he'd once wanted. His friend had found forever love and happiness. As for Hayden…well, he'd learned his lesson long ago.

Still, Hayden didn't begrudge his friend. Deacon had come a long way from the man Hayden had first met several years ago. A long way from the mob enforcer who'd wanted to go straight, longing for a better life that he didn't know how to find. Now Deacon owned the Golden Dream, a very successful resort and casino that was second only to the Chimera in terms of success.

Deacon had also found love and seemed to buy into the whole illusion of it since his marriage. Hayden knew better then to try it himself.

He wished the ending for his own story had been as happy, but reality had a way of making sure the scales were kept firmly balanced. And to Hayden's way of thinking, if you grew up with every luxury money could buy but a father who couldn't seem to love you, then something had to give. For Hayden it had always been the softer things.

"Are you going to go inside or just stand in the doorway?" Deacon asked.

Normally he'd walk on by, but not today. "I'm waiting for the right moment."

"And that would be when?" Deacon asked.

"When you get the hell out of here."

"You didn't leave me alone when I went after Kylie."

"Hey, we had a bet. I had to keep tabs on you," Hayden said. He'd bet Deacon that Kylie wouldn't marry him. It was one of the few times that Hayden had lost when he'd gambled, but he hadn't minded the loss.

"Want to make another wager?" Deacon asked. "Only this time—"

"I'm not looking for Ms. Right like you were."

"Why aren't you, Mac?" Deacon asked. His friend always called him by that nickname. It was a holdover from when they'd first met and Deacon had needled Hayden about being the "Mac Daddy." The big guy with lots of cash.

"You know I already tried marriage and didn't find it to my liking," he said, playing off the incident as if it were nothing more than a minor inconvenience, instead of a life-defining moment.

"But you didn't make it to the finish line, so to speak," Deacon said.

"I got close enough," Hayden said. No woman was ever again going to get him to stand in front of a church full of his friends and family and wait for her. There were few feelings he could recall as clearly as the humiliation and anger that had simmered in his gut as he'd faced all of his guests and told them that the bride wasn't coming.

Was it getting closer to forty that was catching up with him or was it Deacon's happy union?

"That doesn't mean it won't work with another woman. This one looks fine."

"Deacon, stop staring at her ass or I'm going to send the surveillance video to Kylie."

Deacon put his hands up and backed away. "I thought you might want a little of the good life."

"I think I've already got it."

"Yeah, well, if you change your mind, I'm here and I've got good advice."

"On what?"

"Romance."

"I don't need advice from you, Prescott."

Deacon flipped him the finger and walked away. Hayden leaned against the wall opposite the glass storefront, continuing to watch the lady unpack her boxes. Damn it had been a long time since any woman had gotten to him like this. Why did it have to be Shelby?

He couldn't stand outside her shop forever, so he pushed away from the wall and entered.

She straightened and her auburn hair fell in waves down the middle of her back. She had a phone tucked between her shoulder and ear as she pulled items from the open box.

"I haven't seen him yet. I'll check in on Friday like we planned. Please don't call me again."

She disconnected the call, turned on her heel and froze. Her jaw dropped and he knew she'd spotted him. Her face went pale as she reached behind her and braced one hand on the countertop, on top of her cell phone.

He walked through the room with a long, easy stride that he strove to keep nonchalant. He schooled his features and forced himself to treat her the way he'd treat any other businessperson who'd leased space from him. He wasn't a first-rate gambler for nothing. He knew how to bluff with the best and how to keep his emotions under wraps.

But he couldn't resist slipping his hand deep into his left pocket and rubbing the top of his left thigh where he had a tiny tattoo of a medieval knight's fist wrapped around a bleeding heart. It was his constant reminder that he no longer allowed his emotions to be a part of his sexual relationships.

It took a lot of guts for Shelby to come back to Vegas after what she'd done. It took the kind of gall of someone who had nothing left to lose. And she'd not only come back to his home turf but taken up residence in his kingdom.

She was still the most beautiful woman he'd ever seen. But she'd changed. Before, she'd been kind of wild—more untamed. The kind of woman who'd made his dad crazy because she was obviously eye candy.

God, he'd been an ass when he was younger. He hoped like hell that Shelby hadn't been aware of that part of him. But he suspected she must've been. Otherwise why would she have taken the million dollars his dad offered and left him?

"What are you doing here?" he asked silkily.

"I own this place," she said.

God, her voice was still soft and sweet. Everything

he remembered about her was the same. She still looked twenty-two. It wasn't fair that time had been so kind to her. He'd be able to handle this reunion a lot better if she'd gained weight, had gray hair, something like that.

"I meant in Vegas," he said, leaning in closer and putting his hands on either side of her, caging her between his body and the counter. Ten years had passed, but right now it felt as if she'd just left him. That had been more than enough time to get rid of any lingering anger, but seeing her again had brought it all to the fore. He wasn't ready to let her go.

He'd never forgotten Shelby's voice. The way it sounded when she was happy. The way it deepened when she came in his arms. Or the way she'd sounded on the phone during that hurried conversation when she'd explained that she had to leave.

"I'm working," she said now.

"I remember a girl who used to say she'd never work a day in her life."

"I changed my mind. Money has a way of running out."

"Even the cool million you took from my dad?" he asked.

But when he saw the color leave her face and watched her pupils dilate, he didn't have the rush of adrenaline that he'd thought he'd feel. Instead he felt big and mean, like the bully his father had always been.

"Of course it did," she said. But inside, a part of her was aching. It had been easy to forget the implications of what she'd done while she'd lived on the East Coast. Distance had provided a kind of barrier for her.

Shelby Anne Paxton stared at the man she'd almost married for his money. She'd been looking for a rich boy to marry and Hayden had been looking for a nice-looking girl to annoy his dad. She couldn't explain it even now, but there'd been a connection between the two of them that she'd always thought went deeper than his money and her looks.

He'd changed in the last ten years but not nearly enough. He still had a thick head of dark hair that curled rakishly over one eye. He had bright blue eyes that had always been able to see past her defenses, and thick lips that made her remember how they'd felt on hers.

Damn, where had that come from?

"Did you know this was my hotel?" he asked.

"Yes, I did," she said softly. There was no way she was going to tell him that his father had flown to Atlanta and suggested she bid for this location. *Suggested* was really too nice a term for what he'd done. Alan MacKenzie had practically blackmailed her into coming back here. He'd threatened to leak the information about her gold-digging past to several magazines. Bêcheur d'Or was gaining an international reputation for class, and the last thing she needed was negative exposure. But Alan had also dangled a carrot—he'd offered her anything she wanted, within reason, if she agreed. Shelby knew he expected her to ask for money.

Yes, Alan had pushed her to come back, and she had.

But now that she was here, she wasn't sure she should have listened to him. The problem was, she still had an obsession with Hayden. He was the man she thought of late at night when she was alone.

"Then why are you here?"

"Um…" She couldn't tell him the truth. Would he believe a part of it—that she needed some closure and to pay him back for what he'd unknowingly given her by asking her to marry him? If he hadn't done that, Alan would never have paid her the money she'd needed to get started in business. Her exclusive line of boutiques turned a huge profit and were considered a value-added chain to many luxury resorts around the world. All of that was thanks to this man.

"I'm waiting, Shelby. Tell me why you're here. Are you hoping to strike it rich again in Vegas?"

In ways he'd never understand.

He stood before her, seething with anger. But she couldn't explain why she was back. Or that she couldn't stay away once Alan had approached her.

She'd forgotten about the anger. Maybe because of the way she'd left. Their last meeting had been a joyous one. The night before their wedding. She swallowed hard. She'd forgotten about her own emotions and how hard they could be to deal with.

"When you say it like that—"

"You sound like the gold digger you are," he finished for her.

"Not anymore, Hayden. I'm here because it's a smart business move." She'd left him at the altar. Called him from the airport with his father's check in her hand. How was he ever going to forgive that?

"Nice touch with the boutique name," he said after a few moments had passed.

A brief smile played at her lips. Naming the shop with the French word for "gold digger" had been her idea. After all, she'd always been unflinchingly honest when it came to what she was. She'd grown up too poor to pretend that money meant nothing to her. "At the time it seemed kind of tongue in cheek," she explained. "I mean, you know how I started out."

"With nothing," he said. She realized some of the anger had faded from his eyes and he was looking at her with something akin to lust.

Passion had never been the problem between them. She'd always been the biggest obstacle in their relationship. Only after a few years of therapy was she able to see that they probably wouldn't have lasted together even if she hadn't taken the payoff his father had offered. Hayden had been more interested in having the most attractive woman on his arm, and she'd been too interested in having financial security. Their relationship had been very shallow.

"And now you have this," he said.

His aftershave hadn't changed in all the years they'd been apart. Still a spicy, masculine scent that she knew he had custom blended in France.

"What do you want from me, Hayden?" she asked when she realized he was staring down at her.

He lifted one of his hands and stroked down the side

of her face. His touch was gentle. She stood still, fighting the urge to close her eyes and lean into that hand. Hayden had always been so gentle with her.

Something few other men ever had been.

He'd wanted a wife and she'd left him to deal with their friends. She'd always felt guilty about that. She doubted that Hayden wanted her back in his life. Though now that they were face to face, she was beginning to realize that was something *she* wanted.

"The wedding night we never had."

"Sex?"

He nodded.

Shocked, she didn't know what to say. The same sensual spell he'd always cast around her surrounded her now. She felt the force of his will and his desire. She closed her eyes and opened her mouth, leaning toward him before she realized what she was doing.

In Alan's words she was supposed to bring some closure to Hayden and get him ready to find a nice girl and settle down. Now that he was feeling his age, Alan wanted grandkids and for his son to be happy. But Shelby knew Alan didn't have her in mind.

She scooted away from Hayden but he reached out for her again. The years fell away and she was suddenly that trailer-park girl wanting the golden boy once again. And there was a part of her who still wanted that man.

Since leaving Hayden she'd had two other relationships—both with wealthy men—but things had never really heated up. Her fault. She was the first to admit she didn't trust her passionate side. Because the one time she had, she'd lost her heart.

"Are you really looking for sex?"

He cocked his head to the side. "Yeah."

"Is this only a revenge thing?" she asked. Because she realized she wanted to say yes. She'd like nothing better than to go to bed with Hayden, even with all the years and anger between them.

"I'm not sure."

"Thanks for not lying." But then Hayden never had. From the beginning he'd said he was the spoiled son of a wealthy man. He'd been kind of immature in those days but so had she. Hayden had also seemed like a knight in shining armor. Shelby had known that eventually he'd wake up and realize he'd made a mistake in marrying her.

"I'll save that for you."

This was more what she expected. She wrapped her arms around her waist and backed farther away from him. She bumped into one of the packing crates and almost lost her balance.

Hayden grabbed her arm and held her until she was steady on her feet. She swallowed hard and tried not to flinch from his touch. But there was nothing harsh in his touch. Just a gentle hold.

"Okay?" he asked in that low, raspy voice of his that never failed to send shivers down her spine.

"Yes. Thanks."

They said nothing for a few minutes. Shelby tried to marshal her thoughts. Tried to find her balance in a world that was suddenly out of whack. She glanced around her boutique, her gaze falling on the poster advertising Puccini's *Madame Butterfly* at the Met. Slowly she let the familiar world she'd created soothe her troubled soul.

She took a deep breath and stepped away from Hayden. As tempting as it was to fall into bed with the one man who'd made her feel really feminine, really alive, she knew she couldn't. She'd changed from the girl she was. No MacKenzie man was ever again going to make her feel embarrassed about who she'd been.

She'd been afraid of being like her mom and in the end that was exactly what she'd become. Someone who traded on her looks for money...for security. But she was a different woman now. She made her own way in the world. She was Hayden's equal in every way that mattered.

"We can't be together if you treat me, like...well, like I suppose you have a right to. I'm really not into that kind of pain."

"I don't want to hurt you, Shelby. I never wanted that."

She believed him. Despite his seemingly shallow playboy attitude back then, he'd always treated her like a lady. She couldn't really explain it to anyone who hadn't grown up the way she had, but when your mother dressed like a tramp and you had a rotating stable of "uncles" in and out of your life, people treated you like trash. But Hayden never had.

"It's been ten years, Hayden. Why do we both still feel like this?" she asked, realizing that Alan had done her a huge favor by sending her back here.

"Honestly, I don't know."

She tipped her head to the side and acknowledged that despite the years she'd never really forgotten him. "I came back because of you."

He tipped his head to the side, not saying a word, just watching her with that electric gaze of his.

She spoke again. "I can't…move on until I figure out what went wrong between us."

"Hell, Shelby, that's an easy one."

"Please, don't say it again. I wish I had the money to pay your dad back so that it wouldn't be an issue between us."

He narrowed his eyes and walked toward her. "So what do you say to some sort of compromise? You give me what I paid for."

"What your father paid for," she said.

"I paid for it in ways you can never understand."

But she did and it made her ache to realize it.

"A night of sex? I don't think I'm worth a million dollars."

"What about a week?" he asked.

"Sex and money. They were my mom's downfall. I— I couldn't do that. If we're going to try this again, I want it to be a real relationship."

He nodded. She saw understanding in his eyes and she realized that if she was going to find any kind of peace with him, it was going to be through bonds of friendship. She wasn't sure she could risk her emotions with him. He'd made her feel so vulnerable. And she didn't want to be that woman again.

"Have dinner with me, Shel. Let's figure this thing out."

"I…"

"It's just a meal."

"I have a lot of work to do here and a short time to do it. I need to hire staff, finish unpacking." The words sounded like an excuse to her and she knew they were. It was just that even though she'd planned to come back to resolve the past, now that the moment was at hand, she was afraid.

But her running days were over. And at the end of the day, Hayden MacKenzie was still just a man.

Yeah, right.

Hayden entered his office in the casino nearly an hour later. Kathy, his assistant, was gone for the day. The small desk lamp glowed at her workstation. She always left it on for him because she knew he kept late hours. There were two messages from his dad, and one from the star of his European-style revue, Roxy O'Malley.

He dialed the backstage number for the revue venue and got the director. "Roxy called me."

"She's onstage right now. Want me to have her call you back?"

"I'll stop by after the show. Let her know."

"I will."

"Any problems?"

"A few guys were hanging around after the first show but security took care of them."

"Keep me posted."

He hung up the phone, leaning back in his chair. His office had windows on two sides that showed the Strip out of one, and the Chimera's hotel building out of the other. One wall held a bank of security monitors and Hayden crossed to them.

He took the access remote and keyed in Shelby's store. The lights were on but the place was empty. Had she run? But then he saw her. Standing in the shadows staring at something in her hands that he couldn't make out.

He reached for his phone and dialed her shop. He saw her move from the shadows to the counter near the register and pick up the phone.

"Bêcheur d'Or."

"It's me."

"Hayden."

Just his name softly whispered. He saw her hand go to her throat and her eyes close. What was he doing?

"Are you okay?" he asked at long last. No matter what he wanted from her, no matter that he intended to find some closure from their relationship whatever the price to her, he really didn't want to hurt Shelby.

She put her hand on the counter and straightened up. "Yes, why do you ask?"

"I'm watching you."

"How?" she asked, pivoting to see if he was standing nearby.

"On video surveillance."

"I'd forgotten that part of Vegas. So, am I on closed circuit?"

"Why?"

"No reason. I just want to know who's watching."

He hit a switch and turned off access to her shop at every other monitor except his. "Just me."

"Why are you watching me?" she asked. Wrapping one arm around herself, she looked small, vulnerable. Not a bit like the schemer his dad had called her.

"I was debating something."

"What?"

"What would happen if I took what I want from you," he said.

"What is it you want, Hayden?"

"I thought I told you. Revenge."

He saw her bow her head. Even though he was several floors above her and in a different wing of the hotel, he felt the sadness that swamped her at his words. "I want to give you that."

He was surprised. "Masochism your new thing?"

"No, but reparation is."

"Shelby—"

"Don't say anything else, Hayden. Let's have dinner and talk terms."

Two

Shelby wasn't sure she could do it. She stood in the suite of rooms she'd been given in the Chimera to use until the shop was open. She was only here temporarily until the boutique opened in three weeks, and then she'd be returning to headquarters in Atlanta, where Paige was holding down the fort, until their next shop opened in the fall. Right now she wished she was back in her safe little condo in Buckhead, watching television and eating fat-free microwave popcorn. Safe but boring. Those words described her life and she had to admit she was ready for a change.

So, here she was in Sin City with the one man who'd never been safe or boring. And she was hesitating in front of her closet as if it was her first date. The last time her choices had been simpler. She'd set out to catch herself a wealthy husband. But this time she had no idea what role she was in.

She closed her eyes and tried to find the confident woman she'd been until she'd glanced up and seen Hayden MacKenzie staring straight back at her with anger, lust and pain in his eyes. She'd known then that the dreams that had been haunting her had led her back to this place to do one thing. To find a way to give this man peace in exchange for what he'd unwittingly given her.

She had a successful career and the life she'd always dreamed of. But did Hayden? Seeing how deeply her choice still affected him made her want—no, need—to make up for it in some way. If parts of her dream life weren't exactly perfect, well, that was a price she'd happily pay.

She pulled a brightly colored wraparound silk skirt from the hanger and shed her business skirt and thigh-high hose. The fabric was cool against her legs as she fastened it just below her waist. She shrugged out of her suit jacket and tossed it on the chair in the corner.

She had firm breasts so she scarcely ever bothered with a bra. Tonight was no exception. She paired the skirt with a soft white camisole. She took a quick glimpse of herself in the mirror. She looked the way she always did, cool and polished. She tried to fluff her hair up and then realized what she was doing.

Hayden wasn't really dating her. She closed her eyes, leaning her forehead against the mirror. Then she took a shuddering breath. She was strong, capable, and this was the only penance available to her.

Over the years she'd tried to pay Alan MacKenzie back the money she'd taken. Not in one lump sum, as she'd never had that much disposable cash on hand. But in chunks. And he'd always refused, saying that he didn't want her money; he only wanted his son to be happy.

She didn't doubt that. Alan and Hayden had a complex relationship that she'd never taken the time to understand until it had been too late. She'd realized that Hayden had only dated her to needle his father. But she'd been dating him for his money, so she hadn't quibbled.

She was exactly the wrong type of woman for a man with Hayden's future back then. Hayden would never know how right his father had been. Alan had made it clear that he'd tell Hayden every detail of the life she'd hidden from him if she hadn't taken the money he'd offered.

But now… A lot had changed in ten years. Now apparently Alan thought that she could help Hayden. And in order to pull this off she'd have to keep that secret from the man she'd betrayed.

She was dithering and that didn't fit with who she was, so she pushed away from the wall, put on her strappy gold sandals and left the room.

She didn't look back or hesitate. She'd made a conscious decision when she'd come to Vegas. Facing the past had never been an easy thing. She'd always looked forward because the past— She didn't want to go there. Not now.

She exited the elevator in the lobby and glanced

around for Hayden. She didn't see him at first but then found him standing off to one side talking with an extremely attractive blonde.

Shelby realized that for all she knew, Hayden was involved with another woman and really was just using her for revenge. It didn't matter that she'd said she was doing whatever it took to bring Hayden some peace; she knew in her heart she still wanted him.

Hayden had changed clothes as well, wearing a button-down shirt in midnight blue and a pair of faded jeans. On anyone else the outfit would have seemed casual, but the way he carried himself belied that impression.

He glanced up and caught her gaze, motioning her over. The woman he was talking to had the kind of beauty that made Shelby feel like an ugly duckling. Her long blond hair fell past her shoulders and her makeup, though a little heavy, accentuated her classic bone structure.

Hayden gestured for her to join them. The woman glanced over at her and smiled. It was a sweet, welcoming smile and Shelby felt warmed by it.

"Roxy, this is Shelby Paxton. She owns a boutique that's opening here in the Chimera in the next few weeks. Shelby, this is Roxy O'Malley, the star of the Chimera's top-rated revue."

"Nice to meet you," Shelby said.

"Same here. What kind of shop do you own?"

"Lingerie."

"My favorite kind. I'll have to check it out."

Shelby reached into her purse and pulled out an invitation to the grand-opening party. "We're having a little party to celebrate."

"I'll be there," Roxy said. She glanced over at Hayden.

"I'll look into that matter we discussed," Hayden said.

"I'd appreciate it, Hay. I know he could be harmless, but something about him made me leery."

"No problem, Roxy. I'll let you know what I find out."

When Roxy left them, he turned his attention to Shelby. She felt his hot gaze on her, taking in the length of her bare arms, lingering on the scooped curve of her neckline and then skimming down to her feet in the tiny sandals.

She crossed her arms around her waist but then realized she was projecting her vulnerability for him to see. And Hayden was intimately acquainted with some of her weaknesses. She didn't need for him to know that he rattled her.

"Thanks for joining me for dinner," he said. "Can you walk in those shoes?"

"Yes. They're surprisingly comfortable. What were you two discussing?"

"Jealous?"

She tipped her head to the side. "Yes, I think I am."

He laughed. "Don't be. It was only business."

"She didn't seem like just an employee."

"You're right, she's not."

"Is she your lover?" Shelby asked, though she hadn't gotten that intimate vibe from the two of them.

"No. More like a kid sister. I really try to make the Chimera like a family. So many people come here alone and…"

Hayden knew loneliness. It was one of the things they'd both had in common. Something Shelby hadn't had to lie about when they'd been dating long ago. Her mother had always been working, just like Hayden's dad. It had given them some unexpected common ground.

She tucked her hand under his elbow. "You're a nice man."

"Sometimes."

He escorted her out of the main lobby to the escalators that led to the mezzanine level. "Where are we going?" she asked.

"To the stars."

"We're going flying?" This was the man who'd swept her off her feet years ago. He'd offered her the fantasy of romance and she'd lapped it up without thinking of the consequences. Like those sunset airplane rides in his Cessna. He'd taken things that she'd never imagined she would do and made them happen.

"Not tonight. Last year I had a planetarium built. Well, Deacon and I did."

"Who's Deacon?"

"Deacon Prescott. He owns the Golden Dream. We work together on a lot of projects. I thought we'd have a drink under the stars before dinner."

"Isn't that going to be a little awkward with all your other guests?"

"No, Shel. I closed down one of the theaters. I'd rather my guests stay in the casino anyway."

"More money to be made that way, right?"

"You know that money makes the world go round."

"Yes, I do."

He slipped his hand under her elbow and led her through the mezzanine. He was stopped twice by his employees with questions that he had to take. Owning Bêcheur d'Or made her understand how demanding running any kind of business could be. She'd checked in with Paige early this morning and had a conference call scheduled for tomorrow at 9:00 a.m. with the builders of the next boutique in Washington, D.C.

Finally they entered a long corridor that was sparsely occupied. The piped-in music wasn't some generic Muzak but the sophisticated beauty of Wynton Marsalis playing the trumpet.

Shelby closed her eyes and wondered for a moment if this might have been her life had she made a different choice all those years ago.

"Vegas has changed in the last ten years," she said, though she suspected it was the changes inside herself that made the city seem so different.

"Yes, it has."

"Did you have anything to do with that?" she asked to fill the silence and keep her mind off the uncomfortable feeling that maybe she hadn't changed as much as she wished she had.

"What do you think?" he asked.

She paused and tilted her head to the side to study him. She knew without a doubt that he was on the image committee and the development committees for the Strip. Hayden wouldn't chance leaving any detail that could affect his business to someone else.

"Yes. I like how sophisticated your hotel is, but that doesn't change the fact that one block over, the area is still a little sleazy."

"Everyone is looking for something different in Vegas and we like to say we can accommodate any type of poison."

"What about me?" she asked, wondering what he thought about her was dangerous. *What you think of yourself is the only thing that matters.* But she'd never held herself in high regard.

"What about you?" he asked. He pulled her into a small alcove.

She felt secluded from the rest of the world with the wall at her back and Hayden blocking her front. He stared down at her with an unreadable expression and she shivered deep inside, realizing how much of life she'd been missing since she left this man.

Because she'd never been able to really trust a man enough to let him affect her the way Hayden always had. She swallowed against a dry throat and said, "What's my poison?"

"Only you can say. I suspect that it's a mix between the gritty reality of where you grew up and this." He gestured to the ornately decorated hallway.

"What about you?" she asked, not willing to dwell too much on how gritty her reality had been.

"I'm the center ring, master of ceremonies. Making sure that whatever reason—fantasy or desire—you brought with you gets fulfilled."

There was a husky sensuality in his voice. She looked

up at Hayden, into his deep blue eyes, and realized that he wasn't all show and both of them knew it.

Hayden liked the feel of Shelby's arm under his hand. The lobby of the planetarium was actually between his hotel and Deacon's Golden Dream. They'd funded a wing together last year that would enhance the experience for their guests. He also had a traveling Impressionists exhibit down the hall in the art museum.

Most people came to Vegas for a reason and Shelby's was probably just profit motivated, but his gut said there was more. He wanted to know more about those reasons.

Hayden had asked the head chef, Louis Patin, to send up champagne and strawberries for a predinner snack, and one of the hostesses handed a wicker basket to Hayden as they entered. He took Shelby up the back stairs into one of the VIP rooms.

"Give me a minute to get everything set up," he said.

"Can I help?" she asked.

"No. I've got it." He gestured toward the plush velvet covered seats positioned in front of the low wall. "Enjoy the show."

She sat down and Hayden watched her carefully cross her legs, then shift to find a more comfortable position on the chair. The slit in her skirt widened and he realized it was a wraparound type and that only one or two buttons were keeping that silky fabric in place.

He caught a glimpse of her thigh before she pulled the fabric over her leg, covering it up. He sighed and then turned to open their champagne.

She was watching him as he poured the liquid and handed her a glass. The material from her skirt slipped free of her fingers. It slid down her leg. The woman had great legs.

"Why are we playing these games, Hayden?" she asked, running her fingers along the length of exposed skin. The stars had begun to appear on the planetarium ceiling, and soft classical music began to play.

"I wasn't aware we were. We both like to flirt," he said, lightly touching his glass to hers then moving back to regard her. Her flesh looked so soft and tempting in the muted lighting in the room. His own fingers tingled with the need to caress her. He clenched them and sipped the bubbling drink.

"I thought you were the master of ceremonies. Flirting is where we both try to pretend that we're not still attracted to each other."

"Is that what you've been doing?" he asked. Already his blood was flowing heavy and every nerve in his body said screw talking and take her. She didn't want the niceties he put on when he was trying to be a gentleman instead of the gambler he essentially was.

"I've been trying. And not successfully I might add," she said, twisting her fingers together in a nervous gesture that made him realize that it might not be real desire that motivated Shelby. It was the waiting. Not knowing which way things were going to fall between them.

"Why?" he asked, needing to know more.

"I can't figure it out. There's always been something

about you that makes me feel…I don't know, like I'm about to jump off a cliff. I know that it's going to be an exhilarating ride but I'm not sure my parachute is going to open in time."

It was different for him. He'd spent the last ten years protecting his emotions from the women with whom he got involved. It hadn't even been conscious at first, but the last woman he'd broken up with had said that he was the coldest man she'd ever slept with. White-hot in bed but stone-cold out. And Hayden had realized the truth about himself. The truth that had probably been there the entire time. He couldn't do things by half measures.

"We agreed to dinner," he said.

"I know. But I got nervous when I saw you watching me."

"Wanting you," he said.

He closed the distance between them and bent down on one knee. Up close he could see the smooth, lightly tanned skin.

"Do you want me to want you that way?"

"Yes," she said. "Yes, because that gives me something real to cling to."

He shouldn't touch her. Not now. Yet he couldn't help himself. He reached out, scraping one nail along the edge of the material that covered her leg. She shivered, but didn't pull away.

Her hand fell to his shoulder, holding on to him while he touched her. Stroking her was addictive. Her skin was softer than anything he'd touched in a long time. Her muscles weren't hardened by hours in the gym, but softer. It was a very feminine thigh.

Taking the fabric in his hand, he drew it up over her leg and uncovered her. She dropped her hand to the top of her thigh, lightly resting it on top of his.

"Sit with me, Hayden. Let's talk."

He didn't ask why. He knew that she wanted that sweet feeling that had always been between them. The real reason he could never forgive Shelby wasn't so much because of the money she'd taken. It was because of the lesson she'd taught him.

He'd never been the kind of man who had let anyone inside him. Never let anyone see the real man behind the trappings of the spoiled rich-boy facade. But he'd been tempted to let her in and she'd walked away.

"Why'd you do it, Shel?"

She trembled and lifted her hand from his. She pushed away from the chair and walked a few steps from him, looking out over the railing up toward the stars that were playing across the wide ceiling.

He stood but kept the distance between them. When she spoke it was almost too soft for him to hear, but he could make out the words.

"I needed security."

"That's it?" he asked, sensing she was hiding something. He knew then that subterfuge was a big part of what was going on here and it had little to do with sex. It was all about who they both were and who they didn't want the other to see. "Lay it out for me, babe. Because that just sounds like a line."

"I left because I knew that you were twenty-four-carat solid gold and I was that spray-on stuff they use at fairs that wears off after a few days and leaves a green mark."

She turned her head away from him. "I wanted to leave before I left a mark on you that you'd have a hard time getting rid of."

Hayden led Shelby out of the planetarium to a very exclusive restaurant on the fifty-fifth floor of the Chimera. They were led to a private booth that faced the floor-to-ceiling plate-glass windows overlooking Las Vegas. The view was breathtaking. She slid onto the bench and straightened her skirt, looking casual and at ease.

But Hayden wasn't. Tension rode him like a gambler trying to find a winning streak.

Knowing it tightened the knot in his gut. Why did this woman still have a hold on him? And would revenge be enough to loosen her hold?

His mind warned that logic didn't play a part in his actions here and now, but he wasn't really listening with his mind.

The curve of her neck was looking fragile and vulnerable, and he realized that talking about her past was one of her weak points. They'd never really talked about where she'd come from. Perhaps he'd been too shallow to care or too arrogant to think any of that mattered. But now, with the years between them, he realized that her past very much shaped the kind of relationship they'd had.

"Thanks for showing me the stars tonight," she said.

"You're welcome. Would you like some more wine?" he asked.

She shook her head. "Let's get down to business. I believe you said you want to get what you paid for, right?"

When she said it like that he sounded like a bastard. It didn't matter that they both had been acting true to form in those days. He had been a spoiled young man who'd picked a pretty, shy girl who needed him. He'd liked the way she'd clung to his arm, let him pay for everything and make all the decisions. That wasn't politically correct but he wasn't really a PC kind of guy. Despite the money he'd always had, sophistication had always eluded him.

"Yes. That's what I want."

He saw in her eyes that she knew it as well. Knew that she was sitting across from a man who wasn't quite the gentleman he pretended to be.

"You make me feel very feminine when you look at me that way. And I'm not at all used to it. Most men I date are intimidated by me."

"Why?"

"Who knows," she said, but bit her bottom lip.

She knew. Shelby always knew why people acted the way they did. She made it her business to pay attention to those details. "Just guess."

"Because I'm driven to make my company a success. I made too many mistakes when I was young."

"Like you're old now?" he asked.

"You know what I mean. Sometimes I'm amazed at how immature I was when we were together."

He leaned back, resting his arm on the seat behind her. He wanted to pull her closer to him, to cradle her against his body and protect her. But Shelby didn't need him to do that. He imagined that was what she'd been talking about. That men realized that Shelby was an independent woman who made her own way. It was a bit intimidating.

"You've done really well. I read an article about your company in *Entrepreneur.* The reporter said you were one of the savviest business minds he'd ever encountered."

She shrugged the comment aside. "I think he was just being nice."

"Reporters are never nice. He respected what you'd done." Hayden realized he did, too. She'd taken the hand that life had dealt her and rolled with it.

"Well…" She shrugged. It was clear to him that Shelby wasn't there yet. She didn't really respect herself. Had he played any part in that?

"Let's get back to us. I think your dad paid me off so—"

"No, Shelby. I paid that money to you." He hadn't meant to say it but it was best she knew the facts. He wasn't playing around this game—the stakes were high and he wanted to be damn sure Shelby realized it.

"What?"

"Old Alan wanted to make sure I never forgot the lesson he was teaching. He gave you the money, then made me pay him back every cent." His father had always been real fond of that kind of demonstration—one where the lesson was reinforced by humiliation. It didn't help that Hayden had played on his father's biggest weakness: a woman with big soul-filled eyes and an empty bank account.

"Hayden… I had no idea. I'm so sorry. I took the money…well, I didn't mind taking it from your dad because I knew it was how he kept score."

He said nothing. She'd pegged his father easily. It was how Alan kept score and he'd paid off three wives of his own, so Shelby knew that it didn't bother him. Hayden didn't say anything else but he knew that he'd paid for Shelby with more than just money. He'd paid for her with his soul and now he wanted hers.

Shelby couldn't have been more shocked. She'd never imagined that Hayden had ultimately paid for her giving up their relationship. But then she'd allowed Alan to push a wedge between them. Let him threaten her with revealing the secret she'd kept from Hayden. The one she still didn't really want him to know. She wished there were some way to escape the intimacy that he'd created around them. She didn't want to be sitting so close to him while hashing out the past.

In her mind it was easy to pretend that she was noble and wanted to pay him back—whatever the cost—so that he could find some peace from the past. But the reality was, it hurt. She didn't want to flirt with the only man with whom she'd ever really been honest emotionally.

She didn't want to open up herself and him to the kind of hurt that would undoubtedly come. Because she knew that she wasn't going to be able to just give him a week of sex and then watch him walk away.

Hayden put his arm around her and pulled her against his side. She closed her eyes and pretended that this was something else. Something that she'd done without for a long time. Comfort was easy to take from Hayden. He had big shoulders and a solid chest, and he was more than capable of carrying any burdens.

But that didn't mean that eventually the burdens wouldn't be too heavy for him. She turned in his embrace, put her arms around his waist and rested her head over his heart. His hands moved up and down her back, before settling on her hips, holding her close.

His breathing changed, grew heavier. She felt his body changing under hers as well. There was no getting around the fact that sexually they were like kindling and flame. But was that the kind of fire that could be tamed or would it once again consume them?

He brought one hand up under her chin, tipping her head back. "What are you thinking?"

She struggled against telling him the truth. He already saw more of her than anyone else except Paige. Most people she met were content to see only the surface of who she was—a driven, competent businesswoman. But Hayden…he'd known the vulnerable woman underneath. The one who still wasn't sure of her place in the world.

"I'm thinking this is a mess that I made and it's past time I cleaned it up."

"I think we can both carry the blame," he said, stroking her cheek with a gentleness that made her heart beat a little faster.

"Do you ever feel like life is really a great tragedy? Like the ones in operas?"

He didn't say anything, only continued stroking her back. Shelby wondered if she'd said too much. Her life had never been ideal, but comparing it to a tragedy… She wasn't some scared little miss. She needed to stop acting like one.

"I think that in some ways much of our lives is like opera, how operas show the intense emotions that sometimes influence our decisions. Why?"

This was the man who'd convinced her to take a chance and marry him. This soft poet's soul that she'd scarcely glimpsed since her return to Vegas.

"I thought maybe we were caught at the end of the second act. You know, where all seems doomed."

"And that maybe it was time to move on to the third act?"

She couldn't answer. In one of her favorite operas, *Tristan und Isolde,* the third act had them both dying. But for a love that was so true and right that it captured both of their souls, uniting them even in death. Maybe that was the trailer-park girl deep inside her, but she wanted a man to love her that much.

"What do you want from me?" he asked.

That was the million-dollar question. Alan wanted his son happy and expected her to fix whatever she'd broken when she left. Hayden wanted closure and revenge. But what did she want? Shelby had never really figured that out and it was time to. "I guess a chance to make this real."

Hayden could tempt her into believing that if she showed him her soul he'd reward her with his heart. But she suspected if she did that, he'd take the revenge he so richly deserved. She felt the Sword of Damocles hanging over her. Knew that at any minute the hair might snap.

"How could it not be?" he asked in that deep voice of his.

He was right. There was nothing subtle about the man holding her and nothing tentative in him. He was going to pursue her for his own reasons and she had to decide what she was going to do. She knew with bone-deep certainty that she wasn't going to resist him. He was her secret longing and she'd never forgotten him. So now she had to decide. Was she really going to meekly let him take charge of this? Or was she going to meet him on a level playing field?

"I want you, too, Hayden. And I have an offer for you."

"I'm listening." He traced the line of her spine up her back. His finger circled her neck and toyed with the strap of her camisole.

"Let's make this real. Let's say what this really is. I want a chance to get to know each other the way we never did before."

He pulled the strap of her camisole toward her shoulder and then lowered his head, blowing on the exposed skin. As shivers moved down her arm and back, she undulated in his arms, holding more tightly to his waist.

"Okay," he said.

"Okay?"

She couldn't think when he was this close to her. When he surrounded her with his heat, his touch and his scent. She just wanted to close her eyes and pretend that they didn't have the past between them. Close her eyes and imagine that Hayden MacKenzie really could want Shelby Paxton just for who she was.

"I'll let you try to make me fall in love with you. But honestly, Shelby, I don't have a heart."

"Yes, you do. And I'm just the woman to find it." She promised herself she would. There was no problem she couldn't solve once she put her mind to it. She'd figure Hayden out—find out what made him tick—and slowly work her way into his heart, because she knew from hearing him speak of her betrayed that he still had one.

"You might be right. After all, you were the last one to see it."

She shivered and this time it wasn't from his touch. It was from the coolness beneath his words. She realized this time she may have risked more than she'd anticipated.

"Double or nothing," she murmured, realizing that was exactly the bet she'd made. Both of their hearts united and at peace or once again broken.

"That's the kind of gamble I make every day in business, but this…"

"I'm in if you are, Hayden," she said, unable to keep the challenge from her voice.

"Oh, I'm in."

Three

"The only way to do this is to live together," Hayden said while they were eating dessert.

Shelby choked on a bite of her tiramisu. "What?"

He patted her back and handed her a glass of water. He liked the thought of it now. Her living in his home. Shelby there when he woke up and there when he went to sleep. She said she wanted a chance to know him, to seduce him this time. Living together made the most sense.

"You okay?" he asked.

"Yeah. No. I can't think this late at night. I've had too much rich food."

He smiled at the way she said it, but he knew the truth. She wasn't ready to make a decision. Once she saw his home, though, she'd capitulate.

"Come up to my place and just see it."

She shook her head.

He frowned. In the past, Shelby had never denied him anything. But of course, this wasn't the past. And she was a different woman.

"Why not?"

"Because unlike you I need more than four hours of sleep every night. I need a solid eight and I'm tired."

She had a point. His cell had been vibrating with new messages and he saw Raul, his general manager, hanging around the hostess stand waiting for him. Hayden's reality involved work for almost a solid eighteen hours a day. But that didn't mean he was letting this go. "Are you free for breakfast?"

"Just coffee. It takes a lot of work to open a store in three weeks, plus I have a conference call with Paige and the developers for our D.C. project at 9:00 a.m."

He pulled his BlackBerry phone/PDA from his pocket and checked his calendar for tomorrow. He had an 8:00 a.m. meeting with the gaming commission. Followed by a meeting with his roulette-table staff. And he needed to talk to his head of security about the man who'd been sitting in the front row at each of Roxy's performances for the last three weeks.

"What time?" he asked. He'd move some stuff around if he had to. But his schedule was already tight. Why was he doing this? He didn't question his motives, only knew that if Shelby was willing to work toward something solid, hell, he was, too. It felt right, having her here with him.

She shook her head, her thick hair slipping over her shoulder and down her chest to curl over her breast. "I don't know…seven?"

He remembered how her neck tasted, how soft her skin had felt under his touch, and everything in him went on alert. He wanted this woman. Wanted her naked in his bed. He could see her against his gray sheets. A splash of color in his black-and-white bedroom.

She stared at him.

"What is it? Seven isn't good for coffee?"

He shook himself, but he couldn't push away the image of her lying on his bed with a couple of pillows shoved under her hips. Those lush long legs open, inviting.

"No, that's perfect. I'll have a key card sent to your room. Just come up when you're ready." He was ready now. He didn't know if he could wait. If he could let her set the pace for this reunion of theirs. He wanted to take the lead. Get her into bed and push away the past in the most elemental way. To reassert his dominance over her by making her his.

"Hayden…"

"Yes?" he said. He signed the check and slid out of the booth.

"I'm supposed to be seducing you," she said, joining him.

"Do you think Tristan really waited for Isolde?" he asked, reminding her of the opera she loved, the one that he'd let her talk endlessly about when they'd dated long ago.

She smiled. It was all that was sexy and sweet. Much

like the woman herself. "I'm sure he didn't, but he was a warrior."

"Maybe I am, too," he said, putting his arm around her and leading her out of the restaurant. He'd learned some hard lessons when she'd left him. He'd become a different man because of her. He had realized he was no longer the golden boy who had everything handed to him. Instead, he knew, in his heart, he was a man who'd fight for what he wanted.

"I thought you were a gambler," she said.

"Can't a man be both?" he asked, leading her to the bank of elevators. He didn't really want to dwell on his own shortcomings.

"You tell me," she said.

"I already did."

"Where are we going?"

"I'm escorting you back to your room."

"That's so sweet," she said.

He bit the inside of his mouth to keep from smiling. "I'm a sweet guy."

"Ha. Don't think you can put the moves on me and I'll invite you in."

"Put the moves on you? Give me a break. I'm a little more suave than that."

They got in the elevator car. There was another couple already in there who got off on the thirtieth floor. Shelby's suite was on the thirty-fifth. She pulled her key card from her purse when the elevator stopped on her floor.

"Good night," she said, stepping out.

He followed her into the hall. "Yes, it has been."

"Don't, Hayden. This isn't easy for me."

"I'm not pushing, baby. I'm just seeing you home. Something we never did before."

She flushed a little bit. He wondered at the secrets she hid. Her background wasn't like his, and he hadn't pushed her to talk about it. Maybe that had been part of the problem. He'd easily accepted the personal boundaries she'd set because they'd allowed him to make her into what he wanted her to be.

"About that…"

"Don't say anything more. This is double or nothing. The stakes are high, and as you said, you need some sleep. We'll start again in the morning."

He took her key card from her hand and unlocked her door for her, pushing it open. She paused in the entryway, the glow from a lamp backlighting her.

She looked ethereal, with her thick wavy hair falling around her shoulders. Her skin was soft and pink, and that little white top skimmed her curves.

He bent down to brush his lips to hers. Just a sweet salute to the agreement they'd made. But once his lips touched hers, all that fled and he needed more.

She parted her lips and he tasted her sweet mouth. He touched his tongue to hers as he braced one hand on the doorjamb and buried the other in her hair, holding her head still.

He lifted his head slowly. Her eyes were heavy lidded and he saw the first flush of desire on her face. If he pushed now he could have what he wanted tonight, but he knew that he'd lose ground when tomorrow morning came.

He rubbed his thumb over her lower lip before dropping his hand to his side. He passed her key back to her. "Now it's a good night."

He waited for her to step inside her room and close the door and then he walked away. He wasn't really sure what was going to happen with Shelby. He didn't believe in love. Which might be why he'd overlooked the fact that Shelby had obviously kept a lot of her life from him. But for the first time since he'd opened his casino, he felt really alive.

Shelby had set her alarm for six o'clock but didn't need the buzzing to wake her up. Her sleep had been plagued by fevered dreams of Hayden. He'd always been her guilty, erotic, secret dream man. The one she visited late at night when no one else could know.

His kisses had refueled a fire that had never been extinguished. She was restless and edgy when the alarm finally rang. She hurried through her shower and dressed in record time.

Everything with Hayden was exactly the way she'd always dreamed it could be. But in the back of her mind the thought that Alan had sent her here weighed heavily. She didn't know how to bring up Alan without alienating Hayden once more.

Anxious to see him again, she deliberately hesitated in her suite. She didn't want him to know how much she craved him. She wanted to have a little of the control she'd ceded so easily to him last time, some sort of equality. But she wasn't sure how to find it.

The key card for his penthouse apartment had been delivered to her last night, just twenty minutes after he'd left. She held it in her hand. It was the key to something she'd always wanted. Something she hadn't believed in enough to stick around for the last time. But now...

The phone rang before she could complete the thought. She picked it up reluctantly. Only two people would call her here. Paige, her business partner, or Alan.

"This is Shelby."

"How's our plan going?"

Alan's voice was deeper, scratchier than his son's, thanks no doubt to years of smoking. She hated that he never identified himself. She suspected he did it to prove that everyone remembered him.

"You still there?"

"Yes, I'm here. I...it doesn't feel right. I'm here but that's got to be the end of it, Alan. I don't want to be talking with you behind his back."

"Do you really think that my son is going to accept your past? Do you really think that you can make him overlook the fact that we MacKenzies can trace our ancestors back to the first westward migration and you don't even know who your father is?"

His words hurt and made a wave of shame roll over her. Yes, she did think that. Hayden was no snob, and it was more Shelby's business image and sense of personal privacy that would suffer from the exposure. But she knew she had her work cut out for her in changing Hayden's opinion of her anyway. "I'll do whatever I have to." With those words she hung up on him.

Her phone started ringing again but she didn't answer it. The last time she'd listened to Alan, she'd ended up hurting Hayden. Not this time.

It was exactly seven o'clock when she stepped off the elevator and arrived at Hayden's door. She hesitated a minute and knocked. Despite the key, she didn't feel that she should just let herself in.

He opened the door a few seconds later. He wore a pair of dress pants, a blue shirt that highlighted his eyes and a discreetly colored tie and had a phone cradled between his neck and shoulder. He gestured for her to come in.

"Sounds good," Hayden said into the phone. "Call my assistant and set up a meeting for tomorrow."

He disconnected the call. "Right on time. I was hoping you'd come early."

She didn't know how to respond to that. She'd been so needy before that she was afraid to let him see how much she still needed from him. Still wanted from him.

"I had them set up a light breakfast out on the terrace. I'll give you a tour later, if we have time."

She followed him across the hardwood floors through the living room. There was no video equipment or expensive television, which seemed odd to her for a bachelor. The leather sofa and love seat were situated to face a seascape scene on the wall.

Floor-to-ceiling windows lined one wall and there was a bar along another wall and a small poker table set in front of it. The room was definitely masculine in its decor but so comfortable that she immediately felt at home.

"I like this," she said, stopping to take it all in.

"Good. You can change anything you want when you move in except for my poker area. I host a quarterly poker weekend for some of my friends."

"Tell me about them," she said. She wanted to know more about Hayden. She'd been afraid to meet his friends when they'd been together before. Afraid that they'd make Hayden realize how different she was from his set, how she didn't really belong with the golden boy he'd been.

"Well, I've mentioned Deacon. He's a trusted friend as well as a business partner. Then there's Max Williams—we went to the same prep school. And Scott Rivers—I met him when I was bumming around Europe."

She raised her eyebrows. Former child star Scott Rivers was still an A-list celebrity. She hadn't known he and Hayden were friends.

"When'd you do that?"

"After you left."

"Why?" she asked. She remembered what he'd said about having paid the million dollars she'd taken from Alan. She'd never thought about how he'd earned the money.

"I was trying to make the old man give in and release my trust fund."

"Did it work?" But she knew it hadn't. Alan was a stubborn man and he'd been intent on teaching Hayden a lesson. Unfortunately it had worked better than Alan had anticipated.

"No. It didn't. Finally I ended up on the Côte d'A-zur—with no money. I stayed with Scott for a while and then one morning I woke up hungover and out of cash and realized that I couldn't keep living that way. The old man wasn't going to give in. So I went to the first casino I came to and asked for a job."

"Why a casino?"

"I had this idea of showing the old man up."

"Did it work?"

"I don't know if I showed him up, but it gave me an understanding of where he was coming from and eventually it enabled us to have something to talk about."

He led her outside to a wrought-iron table that was set with a carafe of coffee and two plates. "I remembered you liked croissants but I couldn't remember anything else."

"A croissant is fine," she said when they were both seated.

There were also eggs, bacon, sausage and home fries. But she wasn't hungry. She couldn't think about food when Hayden was nearby. She just…wanted him.

"What do you think of the view?"

She glanced out at Vegas. This was the vantage point she'd always wanted to see it from. And knowing that, understanding that she was still that trailer-park girl wanting desperately to escape, she hesitated to say anything else. Because she didn't really know if she wanted to say yes to Hayden because of the view or because of the man.

* * *

Hayden's PDA beeped, reminding him he had to be downstairs in five minutes for his eight o'clock meeting. But he wasn't ready to leave yet.

"What was that?" Shelby asked.

"I've got to go to a meeting in a few minutes," he said. For the first time in recent memory he wasn't ready to go to work. Shelby was more exciting than business.

She pushed to her feet, dropping the napkin on the table. "I need to get to work, too. Thanks for inviting me up for breakfast."

He captured her wrist in his hand, holding her by his side. Her bones felt delicate under his big hand, but he knew that she held all the power. He wanted her. And he'd do whatever he had to do to have her. "I invited you to move in with me."

"I know, but if I do that we'll be in bed together and…I'm not ready yet. I don't want to make the same mistakes we did last time."

"What mistakes are those?" he asked. He'd always figured last time his only mistake was not showering her with presents. But he knew now he'd done other things wrong, too. Frankly, he wasn't sure he'd do them right this time. He wanted Shelby—she was the only woman he'd never forgotten—but he wasn't sure he had forever left in him. His world changed with the roll of the dice or the flip of a card.

"The mistake," Shelby said, "was and would be letting great sex cloud the fact that we don't know each other."

Back then, they'd spent most of their time together naked. He knew he'd been Shelby's first lover and to be honest it had seemed as if they'd been made for each other. He still got hard thinking of the chemistry between them in those days.

"Great sex?" he asked. Maybe he wouldn't have to work so hard to convince her to move in with him after all.

She pulled away from him and wrapped her arms around her waist. That was the second time he'd seen her do that. Why did she? "Trust you to fixate on that."

"It was the only good thing you said." And it was. The sex between them had been great. It had been easy to let sex and lust take the place of friendship and genuine affection. This time he knew she wanted more—but he wasn't exactly sure he would allow it.

"Are you free later on?" he asked.

"For what?"

"A flight over the desert. I recall you liked flying at sunset." She'd never been in a plane before he'd taken her up in his little Cessna. Hayden loved to fly. His plane collection was more extensive now.

She bit her lower lip. "You remember a lot about me."

"Too much sometimes," he said, more to himself.

"I'm embarrassed to say I don't remember the details like you do."

"Why embarrassed?" he asked.

"Because…I was so shallow back then. I was…"

"What?" he asked.

"Fixated on not becoming my mother." She said it so quietly he knew that she didn't want to admit it.

"Are you still?" he asked.

"I think the fear is so deeply embedded in me that I'll never escape it."

He'd never really asked about her family. He'd known that she hadn't had a lot of money—that had been part of her initial attraction for his younger, rebellious self—and that her family wasn't very close, but beyond that he knew nothing.

"What do you like?" she asked at last.

"Pleasing you," he said smoothly. He hoped she didn't realize he was using the same lines and practiced moves on her that he did with all the women he dated. But he knew no other way.

"I don't think so. If we're going to do this…if I'm ever going to move in here, Hayden, we have to have honesty between us."

He rubbed the back of his neck. He was unable to believe she'd called him on his behavior, especially since she had at least as many secrets as he did. "That works both ways."

She swallowed and her face lost color. "Okay, what do you want to know?"

"What did my dad say to make you leave?"

She shivered. He saw her and almost reached for her, but he knew that he used sex as a substitute for real emotions and forced himself to keep his hands by his sides.

"I…um…"

"Just say it. Nothing is that bad. Was it about your mom?"

"Yes. My mom is a stripper."

"Okay. What else?"

"Nothing, just that I don't know who my father is. Mom isn't even sure."

He reached for her then, pulled her into his arms and just held her. She felt small and fragile, and Hayden wanted to take this burden from her. But he knew his dad made a huge issue of ancestry. "I don't care."

She tipped her head back, glancing up at him with those wide eyes of hers. "I do."

He rubbed his hands down her back, not sure what to say. After a few minutes she pulled back.

"Now, what do you really like to do? I want tonight to be to you what flying at sunset used to be to me."

He let her change the subject, lighten the mood because he sensed she needed some distance. "Anything I can gamble on—poker, basketball, skydiving, a fast ride on a desert highway on the back of my Harley, hot sex."

She tipped her head to the side, studying him again. "Wow, that's some list. Let me see what I can come up with. I should be finished in my shop by eight."

Hayden didn't want to relinquish control of her. He knew it was because he'd been burned the one time he'd trusted her. He knew he should let the past go but he couldn't.

She framed his face with her cold hands. Leaning up, she kissed him. There was a lot of emotion, past and present, in her kiss. Her mouth moved over his in a way that was more enthusiastic than practiced. He slipped his arms around her waist and tugged her closer to him.

She lifted her mouth from his and looked into his

eyes for a long moment. What was she looking for in his eyes?

"Let me do this. I want to know the man you've become and show you the woman I am today."

He dropped his arms and turned away, taking two deep breaths to try to get the scent of her out of his nose. But he couldn't. He was inundated with Shelby. Her taste was on his tongue, the feel of her soft skin under his fingers….

His phone rang and he cursed, pulling it out. "I have to go."

"I won't keep you, but what about tonight?"

"I…"

"Hayden, I know that I lost your trust, but let me do this. It's important to me."

He stared at her. "Okay."

She smiled up at him and he felt like a hero. Something he hadn't felt in a long time. But he also felt a little bad that such a simple thing could make her so happy.

"What should I plan for?"

"I'm not sure yet. I'll call your assistant during the day and leave the details."

She turned to leave and then stopped. "You won't interfere, will you?"

"How?"

"By watching me on the security camera or monitoring the calls I make?"

He shrugged. "I can't really monitor your calls."

"And the security camera?"

"I like watching you, Shel."

She blushed then. "I like watching you, too."

"Say the word and we could move you in today."

"Not yet. I want you to ask me after you get to know me."

"I know the important stuff."

"Like what?"

"That we both like great sex," he said.

She laughed and they walked to the elevator. The doors closed and he watched her leave but knew he'd made progress in getting her back in his bed.

Four

Shelby's day passed too quickly. She had no idea what to do for Hayden. But she wasn't giving up. She hadn't come from a trailer park to where she was by being easily swayed from her goal. She wracked her brain as she worked, trying to think of a date that Hayden wouldn't expect but would love.

It was harder than she expected. Why couldn't Hayden be like other men? The men she'd dated since she'd left him at the altar all those years ago. A man who was…not important to her, she realized.

Despite the fact that Alan was responsible for her being in Vegas at this time, she wanted Hayden for herself. She wanted him with her for the rest of her life. The thought scared her because it made every action she took more important.

And though she hated to do it, she called Alan for some suggestions. The fact of the matter was, Alan knew Hayden better than she did. Shelby vowed that would change. Alan gave her the number to the marina on Lake Mead where Hayden kept his yacht and said he'd call in the morning for an update.

Shelby made a mental note to turn her cell phone off before Alan called. She longed for a time when she could be with Hayden and just be herself. The first time she'd been too young and too afraid he'd see what she really was. Where she'd really come from.

Ultimately that had led to her leaving him. This time…well, this time she was balancing between keeping him from finding out that Alan had sent her here and just falling for him.

She thought it was telling that Hayden hadn't mentioned his yacht. She wondered if she'd stumbled on to a private thing he liked to keep secret. From running her business she knew how demanding a career like Hayden's could be. Was the yacht his escape valve? His one place where no one could find him?

She hated the out-of-control feeling. But she couldn't figure out how to be herself and keep Hayden. It wasn't that she didn't think she deserved a man like him. It was just that being back in Vegas reminded her sharply of the girl she'd been. And that girl had too many insecurities.

The phone rang and she finished fastening the leather bustier to the headless mannequin before going to answer it. The scarlet garment had a matching thong and was one of Bêcheur d'Or's top sellers.

"I approve of the outfit," Hayden said, his voice low and husky. She smiled to herself.

"Voyeur. I'm wearing jeans and a T-shirt."

"So I like to watch. That's not a sin."

But his voice sounded like one, a carnal sin. This morning he'd been low-key, a man biding his time, but not any longer. Shelby felt restless inside and knew that Hayden had to feel it, too.

She ran her hands down the sides of her thighs. She'd changed into jeans and a T-shirt in one of the dressing rooms earlier. Unpacking boxes was sweaty, dirty work. But she liked seeing the store come together.

"Would you bend over a little and run your hands down your backside?" he asked.

"Is that what you want?" she asked, surprised at how easily his voice and words got to her.

"Baby, you know it is."

She knew that she was playing a dangerous game with Hayden. On a sexual level she'd never been adventurous, never taken any risks. Ha, who was she kidding, she didn't take any risks with her life.

But now, in Vegas this time, she scarcely knew herself anymore but she couldn't help it. She wanted to be his fantasy. Leaning forward, she ran her hands down the back of her legs, then tossed her hair and glanced around to where she thought the camera was located.

"How's that?" she asked, deliberately dropping her voice an octave.

He groaned. "Perfect. Now go slip into that leather number and do exactly the same thing."

The phone was cordless so she moved over to the mannequin and picked up the red leather bustier from the open box. "Have you ever worn leather undergarments?"

He laughed. "No."

"You'd have to make it worth my while," she said, fingering the supple cloth. In truth she liked wearing leather. It made her feel extremely sexy.

"Uncomfortable?"

"Not really, but they don't hide any imperfections."

"What imperfections?" he asked in such a way that she knew he didn't think she had any.

She shrugged. She knew she had them. She spent the majority of her time sitting in an office working. Though she tried to make it to the gym, most days she didn't.

Her thighs were soft, and no matter how many sit-ups or ab crunches she did, she'd always have a slight swell of a belly. Still, she was happy in her body, it was who she was. She just didn't like to see herself in bright light. Didn't like letting anyone see her looking anything but perfect.

"Don't make me say it out loud," she said carefully. Looks had always been important. Her mother had drilled that into her through Shelby's childhood. "Looks are all a woman has when she's poor," Terri Paxton would say. But Shelby had found that brains were better than looks.

"Okay, I won't. Did you make plans for us tonight?" he asked.

Yes, but she was playing her cards close to her chest on this one. "I'm still trying to come up with something you'll like."

He was quiet for a long minute and she could hear only the sound of his exhalation over the open line. "I like being with you, Shel. I always have."

She hugged one arm around her waist and tried not to let the words settle around her heart but they did. She felt a welling of emotion that she hadn't felt in a long time. "You know the right things to say to make a woman buy leather undergarments."

He laughed again and she smiled to herself, pushing aside the deep feelings his comment had evoked. She had to keep her balance here.

"That was my plan," he said.

"I don't know you well enough," she replied slowly.

"I'll show you. Want to spend the night in the casino?"

"I'm not a big gambler. I like to have something to show for my money after I've spent it."

"Like what?"

"Shoes," she said.

"Shoes? An evening in the casino is better than shoes."

She took a deep breath. "Well, maybe one thing is better than shoes."

"Sex?"

"With you," she said, hanging up the phone. She winked at the camera and put the bustier and matching thong in a gold Bêcheur d'Or's gift bag and placed it on the counter next to her purse.

* * *

Hayden spent the day making arrangements for the World Champion Celebrity Poker Showdown. The televised competition would air next month and the producer and her two production assistants were in Vegas for twenty-four hours to get the layout.

Scott Rivers was one of the best poker players in the world and had been a child star of movies and a television show that had run for fifteen years. He'd grown up on TV and Scott liked to say everyone thought they knew him.

But few did. Even after all this time, Hayden still suspected there was a part of Scott that was kept hidden. Growing up in the spotlight had made Scott something of a chameleon. In fact, Hayden had never seen his friend in a situation that he wasn't at home in.

Scott was one of the few people who'd seen him at his lowest. And that had forged a relationship in which both men felt comfortable with each other. Scott was one of his closest friends and Hayden was glad he would be visiting soon. Also, talking with the television people was a distraction. Seeing Shelby this morning, flirting with her on the phone and watching her like some lust-crazed man…well, it wasn't conducive to work.

His cell phone rang as he entered his private elevator. "MacKenzie."

"Hey, Mac Daddy. You up for poker tonight?" Deacon asked.

"Can't. Maybe next month when Scott is here."

"Next month? How about tomorrow night?"

"I'm busy."

"With whom?"

"Why do you suddenly need something to do in the evenings?"

"Ah, let's just say that it's better if Kylie thinks I'm busy."

"Lying to your wife?"

"No. What are you doing? Dating that redhead in the lingerie store?"

Hayden wished sometimes that he and Deacon weren't such close friends, but the truth of the matter was, Deacon was one of the few people Hayden allowed himself to care about. "Maybe."

"Great. Bring her over. We can all have dinner."

"Can't. We have plans."

"Please?"

"What does Kylie have you doing tonight?"

"Dinner with the Vegas Preservation League. A bunch of wealthy do-gooders."

Hayden felt for his friend. Deacon had grown up on the Vegas streets being looked down on by the very people Kylie had invited into his home. "Sorry, I can't help you."

"Page me at eight-thirty."

Hayden laughed. He knew Deacon might want to leave but wouldn't. He wanted to be with his wife. He was besotted with the woman and wouldn't leave her side in spite of the VPL.

"Later, Deac."

"Later."

Hayden rubbed the back of his neck as he stepped off the elevator. God, he hoped he was never so wrapped up in a woman that he was willing to sit through something like that dinner.

Shelby was waiting for him by his penthouse door. "Are you okay?" she asked.

He dropped his hands, walking toward her. "I am now."

He leaned down to claim the kiss he'd been craving all day. She stood on tiptoe, leaning into his body. He cradled her to him, cupping her face in both hands and angling her head for deeper penetration.

His entire body tightened in anticipation. God, he wanted her. This wasn't a lust thing that could be satisfied with any other woman. He craved her taste on his tongue. Her soft skin under his hands. Her soft curvy body against his muscular frame.

He whispered her name against her skin, skimming his mouth down the line of her neck and nibbling on the pulse beating so strongly at the base. She said his name in a throaty voice.

He bit her gently and she arched closer to him. He licked the spot and then suckled her there. He wanted to brand her as his. To make sure that any other man who saw her knew she was taken. That she already had a man.

She sighed, tunneling her hands into his hair and pulling back from him.

He raised both eyebrows at her. "Please say we're staying in."

"Not quite," she said. Her face was flushed and her lips were wet and swollen. She looked as if he'd done so much more than kiss her. He skimmed his gaze down her neck and was pleased to see the mark of his possession there.

"I figured out something for us to do, but I couldn't catch you before you left your office."

She wore a pair of khaki-colored capri pants and a black tank top. Her hair was twisted up and tendrils curled softly around her face. Her eyes were wide and questioning. Clearly she was unsure if she'd made the right choice.

"Great. What'd you decide? Do you want to take me to a private gentleman's club?"

"Has any woman ever suggested such a thing?" she asked in that haughty way of hers. This was part of the new Shelby. The old Shelby was very pliable. She'd done whatever he said and never stood up to him. But this new woman had a backbone and too much sass.

"I've seen it happen in movies," he said with a grin. She made him happy deep inside where he'd been alone for too long.

"What kind of movies?"

He tipped his head to the side. "Come to think of it, not the kind of movie you'd watch."

"Sex movies?"

"Uh, I'm pleading the Fifth on this one," he said, taking her hand and leading her into his home.

Her deal with Alan had some pluses to it. Shelby had made arrangements to have Hayden's yacht readied for them. Lake Mead was located just east of Vegas and

Shelby had gotten driving directions from the bell stand earlier before going to get Hayden.

Shelby felt a little bit of dread at the thought of someday having to reveal to Hayden that his father was once again behind the scenes manipulating things. She made the decision right then to stop talking to Alan. She wanted to learn about Hayden on her own, not through his father's scrutiny.

She shook off those fears for tonight. The sun was setting and a warm breeze blew through the open windows of her SUV. Hayden had a slight smile on his face.

"Where are we going?" he asked.

"It's a surprise."

"Baby, I've lived here my entire life. I'm not going to be easily fooled."

"I'm prepared for that." She'd spent most of her childhood in Vegas and there was still so much she didn't know about her hometown. Of course, she'd frequented places that Hayden would never have gone to. Places that were saved for the poor and addicted.

"How?" he asked.

She shook off the feelings evoked by her childhood memories and focused instead on Hayden. Focused on the fact that after all this time she was determined to make a relationship work with the man she'd promised herself she'd marry.

She signaled and pulled off the interstate onto the shoulder. The interstate was busy with traffic and she was pleased that Hayden looked a little unsure. She rarely got the upper hand with him.

"This is it?" he asked, glancing at the guardrail and the expanse of desert stretching out toward the mountains. "What could we be doing here?"

To keep from smiling she bit the inside of her mouth as she took the black silk mask from her purse and held it up.

He fingered the silk and when his eyes met hers she saw the heat in them. And shivered. She had the impression that Hayden thought this was the prelude to some exciting sexual adventure.

"Kinky sex on the side of the road. How'd you guess?"

Before she could caution him, he ran the tip of one finger down the side of her neck, his thumb rubbing on the mark he'd left earlier.

"Got anything else in your bag, like a pair of satin lined handcuffs?"

"Maybe. How do you feel about being tied up?" she asked, leaning forward to slip the mask on him.

His pupils dilated, he cupped the back of her head and held her close to him. His minty breath brushed against her. "I'd rather tie you up."

She knew that. He was the kind of man who'd have to be in charge. Her lips were suddenly dry and she licked them.

He leaned forward and traced the line she'd just left with his tongue. Arousal whipped through her body. Her breasts felt full, her nipples tight, and she was so aware that all she had to do was lean forward the tiniest bit and her breasts would brush his chest.

She was shocked at how quickly he'd turned the tables on her. She was the one blindfolding him but she sensed he held all the power. He held her in his thrall and she was helpless.

She bit his lower lip, sucking it into her mouth for a brief second before pushing back into her seat.

"I'm just teasing you. This mask is all I want you to put on for now."

"Ah, baby, if I do this, you're going to owe me."

"Really? What will I owe you?" she asked.

"A dance."

"A dance?"

"Yeah, a nice sexy dance with you in that red leather outfit. Deal?"

She tipped her head to the side to study him, but his words and that sexy tone of voice made her want to do it. "Deal."

He took the black silk mask that she'd brought from Bêcheur d'Or. He slipped it on and leaned back in the leather seat.

The Lincoln Navigator was the same model that Shelby drove at home in Atlanta, so she was very comfortable behind the wheel. Her cell phone rang before she could pull back onto the highway. She glanced at the caller display. It was Paige, and for the first time since she and Paige had opened Bêcheur d'Or, she hesitated, not wanting to think about business tonight.

"I have to get this. Sit tight."

"My pleasure."

She answered it. "Hey, Paige. What's up?"

"Nothing, just touching base to get your take on how the D.C. conference call went this morning."

"I thought it went well. Can I phone you tomorrow to discuss it?"

"Why?"

"I'm kind of on a date."

"A date? With Hayden?"

"Yes."

"Okay, call me in the morning. I want details, and I don't mean about D.C."

She smiled to herself. "Will do."

She hung up the phone and shifted the car into gear.

"Who was that?"

"My partner, Paige. You met her, right?"

"Yes. I like her. You chose well, Shelby."

"Thanks," she said.

He reached over and settled his hand high on her thigh. His fingers traced a random pattern that made her center tighten. She wanted him more than she'd wanted any other man.

"Give me a hint," Hayden said once they were moving again.

"About what?" she asked.

His fingers moved, slipping between her legs and coming teasingly close to her core. She tightened her legs to prevent him from moving any higher.

"Stop, Hayden."

"No. Every time you tease me, I'll reciprocate."

"It's something you like to do."

She shifted her thighs apart, and his touch retreated

but not far enough. She was so aware of his hand on her inner thigh she could hardly concentrate on driving.

"Is gambling involved?"

"No," she said, reaching down with one hand to capture his wrist and move his hand back to the top of her thigh.

"Pretty confident of your answer," he said, turning his hand under hers and lacing their fingers together.

"Yes, plus your sense of fair play."

He leaned his head back. "Don't count on that, Shelby. I'm not always a nice guy. There's a reason I'm a gambler."

"You are so much more than a gambler, Hayden. Don't doubt that."

"Don't let me hurt you, Shel. I'm trying here, but to be honest I don't know how to hold on to something I want."

"Do you want me?" she asked, aware that he wasn't acting at all vulnerable with the mask on.

"Yes, I do."

Her hands shook and she was incredibly grateful that he wore the mask so he couldn't see how deeply his words affected her.

"Then let's make sure we don't hurt each other again."

Five

The soothing scent of the water was the first thing he noticed. Shelby had insisted that he keep the mask on and led him through the parking lot. He felt the wooden planks under his feet and stopped.

How had she known? This was one of his most closely guarded secrets.

"We're at the lake," he said, wondering how she knew about his recent obsession with boating. Not even his assistant knew about the boat he kept at Lake Mead. It was the one thing he'd kept to himself, kept *for* himself and shared with no one. But Shelby knew about it.

She paused next to him. "Are you surprised?"

"Yes. How did you know about this?"

"I can't reveal my source. But it took a lot of time and energy to figure this out."

He pushed the mask up and off, pocketing it for later. He was touched she'd dug deep enough to find this out. "Did you rent a boat?"

"Uh, my source said you had one."

"I do. Follow me."

He noticed she held a picnic basket loosely in her left hand and that large leather bag she called a purse was slung over her shoulder.

He led her to the *Lady Luck,* his thirty-foot yacht. She smiled as she read the name. "Has luck been a lady?"

"More times than not. I always treat her right," he said.

"You do have a way with the ladies."

He helped her on board. Her words echoed in his mind. His way with women had served him well. There had never been a lady he'd wanted that he hadn't been able to date. But the women never stayed. What did that say about his way?

The only constant in his life was the Chimera. He'd spent his life betting on the roll of the dice or taking risks, but that meant that life was constantly changing.

He piloted them out of the marina toward the middle of the lake. The evening was nice and warm and a breeze stirred the short hair at the back of his neck. He glanced over at Shelby, still amazed that she'd taken the time to really find something that he liked to do this evening.

It hadn't been a test for her. But if it had, she'd have passed. That scared him because there was so much he'd forgotten about Shelby. She made the world brighter and more exciting. Even when they were younger, it had been the same. She made him want to take bigger risks—and that was dangerous.

"Ever piloted a boat before?" he asked her. He needed her in his arms, closer to him.

"No. One time Paige and I catered a party for some suppliers that was on the lake."

"Tell me about your business. To be honest, I was surprised when I realized you owned such a successful chain of lingerie stores."

She bit her lower lip. He glimpsed a hint of sadness in her eyes before she turned away.

He scanned the area in front of them. No other sailors. He reached for her, pulling her around to face him. "I didn't mean that as an insult. You just never seemed interested in anything like that when I knew you."

"I know. I was only interested in you and having fun."

"I think it's safe to say we both shared those interests."

She hugged her arms around her waist and stared up at him. "When I left with the money…I thought all my problems were solved. I couldn't believe I had a million dollars. You can't understand this, Hayden, but I never imagined I would see that much money. It felt almost unreal."

"Just because I've always had money doesn't mean I can't understand that. What'd you do with the money?"

"I went on a shopping spree. Then about two days later I realized that everything I'd purchased would be gone eventually and I'd be back in the same boat and…"

He stopped the engine on the boat and dropped

anchor. He couldn't concentrate on Shelby and the boat simultaneously.

"What?"

"I couldn't do that again, Hayden. Whatever else you believe about me, please know that leaving you was one of the hardest things I've ever done."

He traced her jawline with his finger, realizing that in some ways, this strong independent woman was worlds too soft for him. Too innocent. Despite the fact that she'd left him, he knew that he and his father were to blame. When he'd started dating her to get at his father, he'd put her right in the middle of the power struggle they'd always engaged in.

"I know," he said softly. "Tell me how you started your store."

"Well, first I decided to go to college. Since I wasn't going to be using my looks to make money, I figured I'd better use my brains."

"It doesn't have to be one or the other."

"I know that now. But I was only twenty-two. You know, at the time I thought I was very mature. I mean, I knew things about life that other people didn't. But there was still so much I didn't know."

Hayden nodded, realized what she was talking about. He, too, had felt he knew it all as a young man, and in retrospect he realized how little knowledge of life he'd really had.

She walked to the railing, glancing out at the deepening twilight. "I met Paige in college and we were both working in a chain lingerie store at the mall. We had this idea that kind of grew from that. Something more exclusive, more high end. Paige said we needed a French-sounding name because the French know everything about sex."

Hayden laughed at that. Shelby did, too. "Paige is crazy sometimes with the things she says, but she was right. Since we'd both come into our money in unorthodox ways, I suggested calling the shop Bêcheur d'Or. Most consumers recognize the French word for gold and it gave us our brand. Those little gold bags set us apart from other shops, and the rest is history."

"How did Paige come up with her share of the investment money?"

Shelby paused, eyeing him. "She was a wealthy man's mistress for about a year. I don't know the details."

She stared as if she expected a cutting comment, but Hayden had heard it all, living in Vegas.

Hayden was impressed with what she'd made of her life. He was also a little leery of getting involved with Shelby again because she had vulnerabilities that he'd never really explored before. And he didn't want to hurt her again.

Shelby hadn't meant for the evening to get so serious. This night was supposed to be about him not her. They'd had a light dinner and now were sitting on the bow of the boat. She'd removed her shoes, dangling her feet over the water.

"What did you do today?" she asked.

"Meetings and the like."

"Just casino business all day?" she asked, because it sounded as if he was hedging.

"No. I also went to a children's facility that Deacon and I set up."

"What kind of facility? Something for sick kids?"

"No. It's for kids whose parents work in casinos. A place for them to hang out and be safe. Kind of like day care, but for older kids."

"What do you do there?"

"Usually I spend my time climbing on the rock wall. We have a scoreboard that tracks times up and down. A lot of the regular kids like to challenge me."

"Do you let them win?"

"Hell, no. What kind of lesson does that send to kids if you let them win?"

He had a point. "You like it."

He tipped his head and looked her straight in the eye. "I didn't expect to. But yeah, I do."

She'd learned more about Hayden in the forty minutes they'd spent on the water than she had in the weeks she'd spent with him before he'd asked her to marry him. He was a deeply complex man, and a part of her worried she'd never be able to fulfill all his needs.

But she was willing to try. She was falling in love with him all over again. Only this time she knew it was the real thing. Not just a chimera shimmering in the distance. But something real and substantial. An emotion that would last for all time.

Hayden leaned back on his elbows, like some potentate. He was too sexy for his own good. She was still hot and restless from his hands on her in the car. It amazed her how easily he turned everything into something sensual.

"Were there film people in the casino today?"

He arched one eyebrow at her. "Your source is very well connected."

She had to be careful about revealing the things Alan had told her. She wasn't cut out for the kind of intrigue that this type of deception entailed.

"That was the buzz in the buffet," she said, hoping she didn't sound as defensive as she felt.

"I was joking with you. Not accusing you of anything. They weren't film people. The Celebrity Poker Showdown is coming to film here next month."

"Sounds exciting."

"Do you watch it?" he asked.

She didn't really spend much time at home. She was a workaholic who took time for the occasional opera performance and that was about it. "No, I'm really not much on TV. You?"

He shrugged, pushing himself up. "Not too much. I try to watch when I know Scott will be on."

She shook her head at this second reminder of the differences in their lifestyles. "I can't believe you know Scott Rivers personally."

"Should I worry about that? I don't really think of him as anything other than my friend who's very good at bluffing." There was complete honesty in Hayden at that moment and she knew that he didn't view Scott Rivers any differently than he did her. Well, perhaps a *little* differently.

In Hayden's voice she heard the affection he had for the man. She knew from the past and from what she was learning about the man he was today that he had few friends. He was nice to many people but he let few know him.

"Why do you like coming out on the lake?" she asked. He was so at home in Vegas that seeing him out here was almost jarring.

"I don't know. It's just the only time I'm alone. I can kick back and not worry about any of the details I'd have to when I'm at the casino. Sometimes I fish, other times I just drift like we're doing tonight."

"What's it like running the Chimera?"

"Exhilarating, frustrating, fun, a pain in the ass. It's a million things at once but in the end I wouldn't trade it for anything."

"I feel the same about my shops."

He smiled at her. "Are we going to talk business all night? I thought you were supposed to do some wicked seducing."

"Did I agree to that? I think that's your fantasy."

"Let's not quibble about the details."

"Well, I wish I'd planned better. I think swimming in the moonlight with you could be a lot of fun."

"What didn't you plan for?"

"No swimsuits."

"We don't need them."

Skinny-dipping. Despite the fact that she was thirty-two, the thought of it was still forbidden…naughty somehow. And Shelby had spent her entire life following the rules in a game that had always seemed weighted against her.

She pushed to her feet and Hayden stood up next to her. "Did I shock you?"

"Did you want to?"

"Yes. You seem so self-contained, so…untouchable, sometimes I want to shake you up."

He had no idea how much he did. She watched him carefully, her fingers going to the hem of her black shirt. "Will this count instead of the sexy dance?"

"You want to bargain now?"

"Yes."

He scratched his chin. "I'm not giving up my dance, so we'll have to bet on something else."

"What? There's nothing out here but the two of us."

He studied her carefully, gliding forward until no space remained between them. He put his hands on her hips and pulled her fully against his rock-hard body. Each breath he took caused his chest to brush against her breasts, rubbing over her already sensitized nipples.

She struggled to keep him from noticing her reaction. But she could tell by the look in his eyes that he knew she wanted him. He knew she was his for the taking. She pushed against his chest.

He was too used to the power, too used to being in control. Shelby needed to be in charge. Just this once, she thought.

"Last one in is a rotten egg," she said. She kicked off her sandals while tossing her shirt on the deck.

Hayden was a competitor who liked to win so he stripped out of his clothing as fast as he could. Watching Shelby's curvy body emerge from under her clothing slowed him down, however. He knew the moment she realized that he was watching her.

She tipped her head to the side and ran her hands over her breasts and down the center of her stomach. Her fingers toyed with the button at her waistband. "Are you giving me a head start?"

Her voice was deeper than normal, husky almost, brushing over his aroused senses like the whisper of a win in a gambler's ear. The lure was totally irresistible and all he could do was helplessly watch her long legs.

Winking at him, she pivoted away from him and bent at the waist to push her pants off. The thin strip of her black thong pulled tight against the crease in her backside. He clenched his hands at his sides as she straightened.

She glanced over her shoulder at him and pulled her hair free. Shaking her head, she let her hair fall in a cascade down her back. He saw red. A haze came over him and he stepped toward her, but his pants caught at his knees and he almost stumbled.

"I'm going to win," she said, taunting him as she daintily folded each bit of clothing she'd removed. Then she took a leap off the edge of the boat.

Hayden's pants caught on his feet and he kicked them off just before he tumbled over the side, splashing down a scant second before she did. As the water closed over his head, he heard the sound of her laughter filling the air.

Lazily he pushed to the surface, coming up behind her. Reaching for her, he skimmed his hand down her spine. She trembled under his touch.

"I won," he said.

She glanced back at him. "Don't get all arrogant about your victory."

"Why not?" he asked, pulling her closer while he treaded water to keep them both above the surface. The action forced his legs between hers.

"Because there was no skill involved," she said, undulating against him so that her entire body caressed his.

"Then you know that resistance is futile," he murmured against her skin.

She pulled away from him. "Did you say 'resistance is futile'? Isn't that from *Star Trek*?"

"I thought you said you didn't watch TV."

"*Star Trek* is more than TV. But it doesn't seem your cup of tea."

"I went to that exhibit over at the Hilton a few years ago, to see about doing something similar at the Chimera."

"Did the hotel benefit from that trip? Because apparently your legendary charm didn't."

"I beat you once, Shel. Don't make me do it again."

"You can try," she said, and dived. He followed her easily, making out the shape of her white legs under the water.

He caught her ankle and pulled her to him, using a powerful scissor kick to bring them both to the surface.

His skin was too tight and he felt as if he was going to explode if he didn't get inside her soon. But he loved the sensual way she moved. He snaked one arm around her waist and fondled her belly button before cupping her breast in his hand.

"I don't need skill. I have raw talent."

"You've got raw something all right, but I don't think it's talent."

"I'll prove it," he said. It had been too long. Still, he knew he had to take this slow, because despite her teasing, Shelby was still feeling her way in this new relationship with him. And the last time, sex had clouded everything else.

She pushed away from him and dived under the water once more.

Shelby still hadn't surfaced when he felt her hand on his knee, skimming up the inside of his thigh. She cupped him in her hands.

He forgot to tread water and started to go under. Shelby surfaced a few inches from him. "Still going to prove something to me?"

He laughed. This was what had been missing from his life. This element of sexy teasing had been absent in all of his relationships until now. He stroked over to her, capturing her from behind.

She turned in his arms and kissed the base of his neck, nibbling at him and then soothing the ache with her tongue. He tightened his hands on her soft body. He wanted to toss her up on the deck of the boat and bury himself hilt deep inside her. He wanted to bind them so close to each other that they'd never really be separate again.

She lifted her head, her eyes sparkling up at him. "Don't try to tempt me with that smooth voice. I remember it well."

He closed his eyes, inhaling the scent of Shelby, letting the feel of her in his arms totally overwhelm him. He needed her like the air that he breathed and he followed that desire the way he'd always allowed all his cravings to rule his life.

Her wet hair snaked over her shoulders, falling onto his. He liked that feeling, and pulled her closer. He wanted them so deeply intertwined, she'd forget everything except being with him.

Grasping her waist, he lifted her slightly and lowered his mouth to her breast. He traced her nipple with his tongue, lapping at it gently until her nails dug into his shoulders. Carefully he scraped his teeth over her and heard her cry his name. They both sank beneath the water and he realized they needed to get out of the lake right now.

He needed more. He needed it now. And so did she. Holding her carefully with one arm, he swam them both back to the boat and lifted her up onto the platform at the back.

When she would have stood, he stopped her with a hand on her thigh. "Not yet."

Six

Hayden pushed himself out of the water using only his arms. His erection was large and fierce looking.

He scooped her up and stepped over the railing onto the deck of the boat. The remains of their dinner and their clothing still lay where they'd been left.

Shelby was a little embarrassed at her abandon, but there was a sense of rightness about being in his arms that made her realize that they belonged together. A kind of confirmation that she'd made the right decision to come to Vegas to resolve the past and cement the future. She and Hayden weren't finished. Their story was still continuing and she was glad about that.

She wrapped her arms around his neck and shoulders as he strode across the deck of his yacht. His heart beat strongly under her cheek and she closed her eyes, pretending that it beat just for her.

He set her on her feet next to the king-size bed in the stateroom. She was dripping on the carpet but she knew that Hayden didn't mind. He watched her with eyes that seemed to be on fire for her.

"Don't move."

He liked to give orders and she wasn't about to fall into the trap that had plagued their first whirlwind relationship. She followed him into the bathroom area. He bent over to retrieve two thick navy blue towels.

Shelby pinched his backside, then ran her fingers down to cup him.

He glanced up at her. "I thought I told you to stay put."

"I don't take orders well," she said. But she realized that she needed this to be about something more than power. She needed to not get swept away in Hayden but to have both of them get swept away in each other.

"We'll see about that," he said, pushing to his feet.

"Yes, we will see."

She took one of the towels from him. "Stand up and I'll dry you off."

He rose, towering over her. There was a look in his eyes that she scarcely trusted. "I like that idea."

She reached out with the towel but he stopped her with an iron grip on her wrist. "Use your tongue."

She swallowed. Hayden was a dominant lover and she freely admitted that he appealed to her as no other man did. Two could play at this game. He liked to give orders but she knew he wasn't immune to her.

"Close your eyes," she said, softly tracing her finger down the line of hair at the center of his body. The hair tapered down to his erection. She caressed him, coming closer and closer to his erection but making sure she did nothing more than brush it.

She licked the drops of water that still clung to his chest, while he dried her with long, languid strokes of the other towel. She dropped to her knees in front of him, following the trail of water down his strong thighs.

She really wanted to push him beyond boundaries, to push herself further than she'd ever gone before. She lowered her head, letting her breath wash over his erection first. His hands came to her head, rubbing her hair but not holding her or pulling her closer.

She tipped her head back and looked up at him. His skin was flushed with arousal. His breaths were rapid and his pupils dilated.

"Hayden, can I…?"

"Only if you want to."

She definitely wanted to. He felt like satin under her fingers. She lowered her head and ran her tongue up and down his length. Taking her time, she tasted him and discovered the different nuances of him. Reaching between his legs, she cupped his sac, massaging it in the palm of her hand as she took him fully into her mouth.

She sucked him deeper in her mouth, felt his body tighten as she worked up and down his length.

She tasted a salty bit of his essence before he pulled her away and lifted her to her feet.

He carried her into the bedroom, cradled in his big

arms, then slowly lowered her to her feet. She loved the feel of his solid frame against her. He wrapped his arms around her, anchoring her to him with his hands on her back.

He lowered his head slowly and she was consumed by the fire that he effortlessly brought to life inside her. She rose on tiptoe to meet his mouth. She loved the way he kissed her, as if he had all day and wouldn't stop until he'd explored every one of her secrets. She wanted to know him the same way. Reaching up, she took his jaw in her hands and held him still.

She traced the seam of his lips with her tongue, tasting him with small delicate darts. His hands on her back tightened but she didn't hurry. He always seemed so in control. What would it take to rattle him? she wondered.

Slipping her tongue past his lips, she ran it over his. She stroked her way into his mouth before retreating and coming back again.

He groaned and his erection pulsed between them. She felt him growing even harder against her belly and reached between them to enfold him in her grasp.

Not about to be outdone, Hayden placed her on the center of the bed. His hands made long strokes down the center of her body, lingering over her full breasts. He circled her nipples with the tip of his finger. She arched her shoulders, wanting to feel his mouth on her.

"Hayden, kiss me there."

"Yes, baby." He lowered his head and took her nipple in his mouth, suckling at her strongly as she cupped the back of his head, holding him to her.

He rubbed small circles around her belly button before delving lower. His fingers separated her. As he slipped one finger into her creamy warmth, her legs moved restlessly on the bed.

He slid a second finger inside her and brought his thumb down to rub her with a small up-and-down movement that made her want to scream; it felt so good. His fingers thrust in and out of her body and she was arching into him, needing more.

Everything in her body focused on his hand between her thighs and his mouth on her breast. He thrust slowly, driving her up toward a pitch until everything in her body tightened and she knew she was going to come.

Suddenly her entire body clenched and she called out his name long and low. She smiled up at him and she felt a sense of rightness. She wrapped her arms around his head and held him to her.

Hayden waited until Shelby's body stilled before he pushed himself up on his elbows to stare down at her. She smiled at him. Her lips were swollen and still wet from his kisses. Her nipples poked into his chest and though he'd satisfied her, he knew she wanted more.

He needed more as well. Once was never enough for Shelby and him. He freely admitted that only when he was lying between her legs, buried deep inside her body, did he really feel as though he was seeing the real woman. She had no chance to put up barriers then.

He set about arousing her again. Sweeping his hands

down her body. Using his mouth to trace the same path. Slowly building her once again to fever pitch.

She didn't lie passively under him but caressed his back and buttocks. Skimmed her hands over him and then scraped her nails in patterns everywhere she could reach. When he could wait no longer, he kissed his way up her body, lingering at the base of her neck. He sucked against her sweet flesh and bit softly until she was moaning his name.

"Open your legs."

His voice was gruff, guttural even. She'd pushed him past his boundaries. When she did as he asked, he settled his weight over her. Taking her hands in his, he stretched them up over her head, forcing her fingers to curl under the headboard mounted on the wall.

"Don't let go."

She nodded.

He lifted her legs and paused at the entrance of her body. The tip of him slipped inside her. She was so wet and so ready. Her body tightened around him as he entered her. He cursed and pulled out. "Are you on the Pill?"

She shook her head. He didn't want to use a condom; he knew he was free of any diseases and wanted to feel her wrapped around his erection, but he couldn't chance pregnancy.

He pushed off the bed and went into the head and found the box of condoms he kept in the medicine cabinet. He grabbed one, sheathed himself before returning to the stateroom.

Shelby hadn't moved. Her arms were still above her

head, holding the headboard. She was so beautiful to him in that moment, caught up in the feelings he'd brought to her, that he paused to watch her.

"Baby," he said between clenched teeth. He dropped to his knees near the bed. Starting at her neck, he nibbled his way down her body. Lingering over her pretty breasts, he circled the plump globes and left her nipples untouched.

She shifted her shoulders to try to move her nipple to his mouth. He allowed her to get closer, licking the tip before turning his head to her other breast and slowly exploring it.

He slid his hand down her body. Her earlier orgasm had left her body flushed and sensitive to his fingers. She was wet and creamy and he used her juice to coat his fingers, bringing them up to her nipples and rubbing her own moisture on them.

She craned her neck to watch him. He, too, was helplessly fascinated by the sight of his large fingers sliding between her thighs and entering her body.

"Hayden, I can't wait much longer."

"Yes, you can," he said, levering himself on the bed and over her.

He settled between her open legs, taking his erection in his hand and rubbing it up and down her center. He pressed it to her little bud until she tightened her thighs around him and her hips jerked upward.

"Not yet, Shelby. Hold on, baby. Wait for me."

She closed her eyes, breathing deeply, and he knew he'd pushed further than he'd intended to tonight. Putting his arms under her thighs, he lifted her legs, opened her fully to him and entered her. Slowly he filled her until he was seated hilt deep.

Her brilliant eyes opened and she watched him take her. For a moment he remembered the first time he'd taken Shelby. He'd been her first and it had been a surprise. She'd been as openly candid about her appreciation of him and his body then as she was tonight.

Her muscles tightened around him as he pulled back for a second thrust. Her hands gripped the headboard so tightly that he knew she was close. He wanted them to come together this time.

His own orgasm was almost on him. He hurried his pace, thrusting deeper and deeper into her. Finally he felt that telltale tingling at the base of his spine.

"Now, baby."

She came at once, her body tightening around him like a wet, hot glove. He emptied himself into the condom, wishing he'd been able to empty himself into her womb. He wanted to claim her. To stake his claim and make sure that no one—man or woman—ever doubted that Shelby belonged to him.

He collapsed on top of her, spent from the powerful climax. He nestled closer to her breast, idly sucking on one nipple. Her arms wrapped around him and he shifted his weight to the side so that he didn't crush her.

He felt as if he'd found his home. That disturbed him deep inside because he hadn't realized that he'd been searching for one until this very moment.

* * *

Shelby didn't want to wake up. She saw the sun shining across the bed, but the feel of Hayden's arms around her was too good to give up. Even to the reality of morning. How many times had she dreamed of him holding her this way only to wake alone once again?

But she wasn't one to hide from reality. And she knew this morning he was real, not a figment of her hungry soul. But this time she had to deal with her own guilty conscience. Deal with the fact that she had gone behind his back to seduce him with the things he loved.

Her thighs and breasts were pleasantly sore from last night. She was a little scared at the intensity of their lovemaking.

She'd enjoyed herself, no doubt about that, but he'd made her feel vulnerable. She didn't like that. She was a business owner—not exactly an occupation for wimps. She was used to dealing with her fears head-on and would deal the same way with this one, too.

Rolling over and opening one eye, she found herself nose-to-nose with Hayden. His eyes were wide open and the most arrogant male grin split his face.

"What are you smiling about?"

"You, here with me," he said. Leaning down, he kissed her.

It was the slow kind of kiss that didn't put any pressures or demands for more. She felt precious to him. It made her realize how vulnerable she was once again to Hayden. Before, she hadn't really loved him, but this time he was so much more to her than a wealthy man.

Now she was starting to know him, to know that he was constantly going. A moving ball of energy. And that he liked to bet on anything and everything.

She tunneled her fingers through his chest hair, caressing his warm, bare skin. She wanted to snuggle closer. To sink into him until they were just one person and then didn't have to face the day apart.

He lifted his head. "We have to get back. I can't believe I left the casino this long without checking in."

He propped himself up on the headboard and she blushed as she remembered how he'd made her hold on to it until she came in his arms.

He saw her color and shook his head, tugging her into his arms. "Thank you."

"For…?"

"Last night. It was…incredible, Shel. I wish our first time had been like that."

"I don't."

"Really? I've always regretted that I took you too quickly that first time."

"I don't. You were perfect, Hayden. And I don't think we could have handled last night before. We were both…"

"Both what?"

"I can't speak for you but I was pretending to be someone else. Hoping you wouldn't notice."

"Why?"

"Why what?"

"Why were you pretending?"

"Because I wanted a rich boy to marry me and normally you wouldn't have looked twice at the real me."

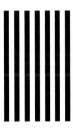

NO POSTAGE
NECESSARY
IF MAILED
IN THE
UNITED STATES

BUSINESS REPLY MAIL
FIRST-CLASS MAIL   PERMIT NO. 717-003   BUFFALO, NY

POSTAGE WILL BE PAID BY ADDRESSEE

SILHOUETTE READER SERVICE
3010 WALDEN AVE
PO BOX 1867
BUFFALO NY 14240-9952

Play the Lucky Hearts Game

and get...

2 FREE BOOKS
and a FREE MYSTERY GIFT...

yes! YOURS to KEEP!

I have scratched off the silver card. Please send me my *2 FREE BOOKS* and *FREE mystery GIFT*. I understand that I am under no obligation to purchase any books as explained on the back of this card.

Scratch Here!
then look below to see what your cards get you...
2 Free Books & a Free Mystery Gift!

326 SDL EEXW   225 SDL EEWM

FIRST NAME   LAST NAME

ADDRESS

APT.#   CITY

STATE/PROV.   ZIP/POSTAL CODE   (S-D-02/06)

Twenty-one gets you
2 FREE BOOKS
and a *FREE MYSTERY GIFT!*

Twenty gets you
2 FREE BOOKS!

Nineteen gets you
1 FREE BOOK!

TRY AGAIN!

Offer limited to one per household and not valid to current Silhouette Desire® subscribers. All orders subject to approval. Please allow 4-6 weeks for delivery.

"Yes, I would have," he said.

"You might have looked but you wouldn't have proposed. I know that firsthand."

"Because of your mom?"

"Yeah. She's never been married."

"Where is she now?"

"Arizona."

"Do you keep in touch?"

"No."

"Why not?"

"She's part of what I was running from when I left, Hayden."

"Aren't you ready to stop running?" he asked.

She couldn't answer that. She thought about her mom a lot. Her mother wrote her a letter once a month and Shelby never wrote her back, but she read those letters over and over and regretted that she'd been so ashamed of herself and the woman who raised her that…sometimes she didn't like herself very much.

Hayden was right, but Shelby didn't know how to bridge the gap she'd forced between herself and her mom. He hugged her closer, his hand coming to rest over hers. He twined their fingers together and then brought her hand to his lips and kissed her.

"Yes, it is time to stop running," she answered finally. "That's part of why I came back here."

"I know you didn't come back because of money."

"Well, I kind of did. The Chimera location is going to make Bêcheur d'Or a lot of money."

"That's business."

"Yes, it is."

The covers slipped lower on his hips. God, she could stare at him all day. She noticed a tattoo on the top of his left thigh. "What's this?"

He covered the tattoo with his hand. "Nothing."

"No secrets, remember?"

He sighed and she realized that though she thought she was coming to know Hayden, he was still a mystery.

He slid his hand away. She bent closer looking at his tattoo. It was a knight's fist, gripping a bloody heart.

Instantly she knew that he'd gotten it after she'd left. She realized that she'd made a huge mistake. But she couldn't decide if sleeping with Hayden last night had been a bigger one than leaving him all those years ago.

Seven

Hayden strode through the main casino two nights later feeling like a gambler riding a streak of luck that just wouldn't quit. Shelby had shown up at the children's facility yesterday afternoon and had given him a run for his money on the rock wall. They'd had a lot of fun and she'd gotten the girls together to compete against the boys.

Last night he'd taken her up in his old Cessna, the same one he'd had when they were dating. They'd flown out over Hoover Dam and Shelby had mentioned that she'd been thinking about going to Arizona to see her mom. Hayden felt as if this time he was really getting to know Shelby.

The sounds of the bells and whistles of the slots and

the rolling of the roulette wheel always excited him, but seeing Shelby standing at a blackjack table, holding one of those small Bêcheur d'Or gold bags, excited him even more.

She still wouldn't move into his penthouse but he contented himself with the fact that she denied him little else. Like tonight. He wanted to show her his world. Wanted her to experience what life was like in the casino and though she said she wasn't much on gambling, here she was. Waiting for him.

She glanced up as he approached, smiling sweetly at him, and it was the sweetness that wrapped around him, stopping him in his tracks mentally. This thing with Shelby was the kind of risk he never took outside of gambling. But he couldn't stop it.

He approached the table and noticed that Rodney, one of his best dealers and longest employees, was the dealer. "Evening, Rodney. You treating my lady nicely?"

"I am, sir, but the cards…not so much."

Shelby laughed a tinkling sound that lit the dark places of his soul and made him want to keep her happy always. "I am the worst player ever. Isn't that right, Rodney?"

He shook his head. "I've seen worse."

"I think he's just being nice."

"Maybe you need some expert help," Hayden said. He took some chips from his pocket and placed them on the table in front of Shelby. She sat perched on the high stool but was still shorter than his six-two frame. Two other players joined the game, but Hayden scarcely noticed them.

He wrapped his arms around Shelby and looked over her shoulder as she picked up her cards. She had the queen of diamonds and a two of spades.

Hayden signaled Rodney for one card, which he dealt faceup. The card was a nine of diamonds. Shelby won.

She squealed and turned in his arms to kiss him. She won the following three hands, still with Hayden standing behind her. "Thank you. I think you're my good-luck charm."

"Ready to try it on your own?" he asked. He wanted to be more than her good-luck charm. He wanted her to move into his house. To sleep with her every night in his bed and wake up with her every morning. He doubted winning a few hands of blackjack was going to sway her.

"Yes. I think I've got it now."

Hayden grabbed an empty stool from a nearby table and joined the play. Shelby lost the first and second hands. Finally she tossed her cards on the table and picked up her winnings.

"Giving up?"

"I don't want to lose all your money," she said, handing the chips back to him.

"They're just chips."

"No, they aren't. I know that you're going to think— I just can't take money from you." She picked up her big leather bag and the small gold lingerie shopping bag.

Hayden pocketed the chips and nodded goodbye to Rodney. This wasn't what he'd planned. He wasn't the most sensitive guy in the world, but he knew that Shelby was telling him something that had to do with more than gambling.

Suddenly all the pieces came together. He realized that while he was dealing with the fact that she'd taken the money and left, she was dealing with the fact that his money, any of it, represented paying her off again.

"Come on." He took her hand and led her out of the casino.

"Where are we going?"

"I wanted to take you to see Roxy's show tonight. We never do anything that's really Vegas."

"Everything with you is Vegas, Hayden."

He tucked his hand under her arm and led her to the theater where Roxy performed. Hayden had a private box where they sat and watched the show. Shelby seemed to really enjoy it, but afterward she was still quiet and he knew that money was still an issue between them. That he'd been insensitive earlier. He still had no idea how to fix it.

"What's next?" she asked.

He had nothing else planned. But he knew that he had to get her away from the casino and taking her back to his penthouse didn't seem right. He needed to get her out of here, to find a way to take that melancholy from her. Somehow he was responsible for it and didn't really know why.

"Let's go someplace a little quieter so we can talk."

"About what?" she asked, but stood and grabbed her shoulder bag once again. He handed her the small gold lingerie bag, not willing to let her leave that behind.

"Luck and Vegas."

"Well, I think we've established I'm not lucky."

"Not at cards," he said, draping his arm around her waist and pulling her into the curve of his body. He shortened his stride to match her shorter one and used his body to protect her from the throng rushing to get to shows or casinos.

He led her out of the casino into the night. The pool and waterfalls were off to the left, but to the right was a small box-hedge maze, and nestled in the far back corner was a padded bench and gazebo.

"Where are we going?" she asked. Her eyes were weary and he knew he didn't want to stare into them anymore.

"It's a surprise," he said, taking from his pocket the black silk mask she'd used on him days earlier. He'd been carrying that damn thing around, tormenting himself with the different ways he wanted to use it with her.

She laughed as he slid the mask over her eyes, fastening it in the back. Leaning down, he brushed his lips over hers. She sighed and opened her mouth for him. She snaked her arms around his waist and laid her head on his chest right over his heart. And he could do nothing but hold her. To make this moment an oasis in two lives that had seen too much chaos and hurt.

The sensation of being blindfolded was difficult to adjust to. Shelby already felt vulnerable from realizing that she was losing Hayden's money in the casino. Sure, she knew it wasn't a lot of money, but still it was the principle of the matter. She'd vowed before she left Atlanta that this time she wasn't taking any money from Hayden. She meant to keep her word—even if it was only given to herself.

After trading herself so cheaply to Alan MacKenzie, Shelby had taken a hard look at herself and her life and she'd promised to never be in that position again. To never be vulnerable to any man. So how exactly had she ended up here—blindfolded with only Hayden's warm hand in hers to guide her through an unfamiliar world?

Panic raced through her. She heard people moving around her and felt as if she was ten again at Meredith Nelson's birthday party. Meredith and the other girls had all disappeared when Shelby had donned the pin-the-tail-on-the-donkey mask. When she'd pulled it off, she'd been left all alone. Standing there in the secondhand dress her mother had purchased on the way to the party. Tears burning her eyes, secure in the knowledge that she wasn't like other kids and would never fit in.

She felt that way again. Being back in Vegas brought all the old insecurities to the surface. It had to be the money thing. Money always triggered that same gut reaction. The blindfold was too much. She reached for the mask.

He caught her fingers, holding both of her hands easily in his grip. "Shh, baby. Don't panic. I'm right here."

"I know I did this to you, but I don't think I like it," she said.

He leaned down and whispered into her ear, "You look so sweet and sexy. I like the fact that I'm responsible for you. I have to protect you. Will you let me do this?"

"I'm a grown woman, Hayden. I don't need a man to protect me."

"Do this for me, please."

He never said please. She nodded her head. She'd try for him, because he'd done it for her without any complaints. But then she doubted he'd ever been in any situation where he wasn't comfortable.

"Are you still upset from the blackjack table earlier?"

She had no response to that. No idea how to respond and still preserve what she now knew was her own illusion that she'd fooled him. The show had been nice but all she felt while she'd been sitting there in the dark was that once again she was in the land of make-believe. Surrounded by people who were pretending their real lives didn't exist.

She felt the warmth of his fingers feathering up her arm, rubbing gently against her skin, wanting her to relax.

"What is going on tonight?" he asked, murmuring his words against the top of her head.

"I don't want you to think I'm after your money," she said, blurting out the words. Then she groaned. She'd never meant to say that.

"Honey…"

"Don't. Let me continue. I'm never going to have as much money as you do. And we'll never really be social equals. But—"

He stopped the wild flow of words with his mouth. His lips moved over hers with surety and strength, making her feel as if everything was irrelevant except him touching her.

He lifted his head but dropped several small nibbling kisses on her neck before taking her hand in his again. "Follow me."

She bit her lip and let him tug her along. She realized that her panic with the mask wasn't only due to the insecurity she'd felt earlier but also had to do with trust. She didn't trust herself. Didn't trust that the woman she'd become was real. Didn't trust that she'd really left behind the young girl she'd been.

Did she trust Hayden? She hadn't when she'd been twenty. But now…? She'd trusted him with her body; she'd set up her shop here based on the success of his casino. Obviously she was leaning that way, but to have the choice taken from her… To have to trust him to protect her while she couldn't see wasn't something she'd been prepared to do.

He stopped walking. She heard him pushing some buttons and then the release of a gate. She was surrounded by the scent of roses and night-blooming jasmine. Hayden wrapped his arms around her waist and pulled her back so that she was sitting on his lap. He nibbled at her neck and she surrendered to the feelings he always aroused in her.

"What's in that little bag?" he asked.

"What little bag?" she asked, turning on his lap so that she rested her head on his shoulder. His aftershave was strong at his neck. She scraped her teeth across the nerve-rich area and felt him stir under her hips.

"You know very well which bag I'm referring to," he said.

His hands roamed up her torso, settling over her breasts. He palmed both of them and she felt them swell and grow heavy under his touch. She reached for the buttons on his shirt, finding them and releasing the top three until she could slip her hand under the cloth and feel his strong, warm pecs. She scraped her fingernail in a random pattern over him and felt his muscle flex under her.

"Stop distracting me. I want to know what's in that bag. I never did get to see you in the red leather."

His thumbs were tracing her distended nipples through the material of her blouse. It felt so good that she couldn't speak for a minute.

"I know. I figured since you were so big on competition, I'd provide you with your own leather."

He groaned. "Damn, woman, I'm not wearing leather underwear."

"Come on. I'll make it worth your while."

"Like you did with the stripping contest?" he asked. His hand was on her waist and then she felt him pulling her shirt slowly up.

She panicked, gripping his wrists. "Hayden, we're in a public place, aren't we?"

He stopped though she knew he was stronger than her and could have pushed her shirt up despite her protests.

"It's time to decide if you trust me or not."

She felt a million things at once—nervous, excited, aroused and a little bit upset that she was so aroused. She shifted on his lap, pressing her thighs together and wondering if she could pretend this was just about sex.

But she knew it wasn't. Hayden wanted her trust and if they had any chance of moving forward, she had to give it to him.

With a sigh, she dropped her hands, knowing that Hayden would always keep her safe. It was him trusting her that had always been the issue. She acknowledged she'd never given him a chance to really trust her because she'd been lying to him. But this time Shelby realized she needed to learn to trust herself and stop lying about what she'd been running from.

Hayden knew they were completely secluded here. The garden was his private place to escape from the busy casino. He'd deactivated the cameras to this section and opened the security gate earlier. They were now in a private section of the maze. She was perfectly safe.

He knew he was pushing her, but couldn't help himself. He wanted—no, needed—to stake his claim on her and he wasn't going to wait any longer. Making love to her two nights ago had made the fact that she didn't trust him into a sharp ache. He knew he'd done little in the past to earn her trust, but this time…this time he was determined to do things right.

She let go of his wrists and he slipped his hands under her shirt. Her stomach clenched as he moved his hand over her. She turned to straddle him, draping her thighs over his, and held him with a fierceness that felt right in his soul.

Slowly, inch by inch, he peeled her shirt up and over

her head. He let his hands trace down the center of her body, stopping to free the front clasp of her bra as they went. She wore a pale pink bra with lacy demi-cups.

"I love your underwear."

She smiled at him and he couldn't resist kissing her one more time. With the mask on, her skirt up around her thighs, her shirt gone and that bra open, she looked like a fantasy come to life.

"Offer your breasts to me," he said.

She ran her hands up her stomach, slowly caressing her own skin, and he realized that Shelby was becoming more comfortable. She covered both of her breasts with her hands, then slowly peeled back the lace to reveal her pink nipples. She cupped her breasts, lifting them toward him. Her hand encircled the bottom and sides but left a small gap between each finger.

With his tongue he traced the gap and felt her hands tighten as he got closer to her nipple. He teased her by outlining the areola first then laved her entire nipple.

He attended to her other breast with the same care. He couldn't stop touching her, needed to caress more of her skin. He loved the way she felt as arousal spread throughout her body. Her hips shifted on the bench. Her hands moved restlessly over her own body, reaching out to hold his head to her as he scraped his teeth down her side.

"Lift your skirt for me," he said, his hands busy at her breasts.

The fabric of her skirt was gossamer light, as he'd noticed when they'd walked through the casino earlier. Ever since then he'd obsessed about it.

Slowly she brought her skirt upward to reveal her thighs and then the matching pink lace panties. Her tight auburn curls were visible under the light material.

He leaned back to study her. Awed that she was his. And she was his no matter how stubborn she was about living with him. Shelby belonged to him. A red haze settled over him and he was determined to prove it to her.

He set about arousing her using every bit of knowledge that he had but couldn't remember where he'd gained it. All other women dropped away. The experiences he'd had with them were only to enhance what he had with Shelby now.

He tugged on her panties, and she obliged by removing them. When she came to him again, he parted her with his thumbs before lifting her to taste the engorged bud he'd uncovered. He suckled her gently, her hips bucking, her hands fluttering to his head to hold him closer.

He brought her to the edge then backed off. He wanted to build a fury within her so that she'd feel the way he did. Out of control.

He kissed her stomach and dipped his tongue into her belly button. He skimmed his hands over her breasts, rubbing them in a circular motion.

Her hips lifted into his chest and he felt her moisture there, realizing he couldn't wait any longer.

"Hayden?"

"Yes, baby?" he asked. Lowering his hands between their bodies, he unzipped his pants and released himself. He slipped on the condom he'd put in his pocket before joining Shelby earlier.

He pulled her forward so that her hips were fitted to his. Now her back was arched and her skirt was still between them.

He grasped her waist and lifted her up. "Hold on to me."

She wrapped her arms around his shoulders, her legs around his waist. Hayden loved the feel of her soft skirt against his stomach and erection. He reached between them, parted her with one hand and guided himself to her entrance with the other.

He thrust upward, going as deep as he could. Shelby's nails scored his shoulders. Her breasts rubbed against his chest. Nothing had ever felt better than the wet heat of her wrapped around him.

She rocked against him again and again and Hayden leaned down, wanting to demand answers from her. But he couldn't. Emotions swamped him as he felt the telltale tingling at the base of his spine signaling that his release was imminent. He slowed his pace.

"Faster. I'm so close," she whispered in his ear.

He put his hands on her hips and thrust up into her as he ground her down against him. He heard her breath catch once and then twice and then a long, low moan as her orgasm washed over her.

He came a second later. He cradled her close to his body, very aware that even if it wasn't wise he was falling for Shelby Paxton, again.

Eight

Shelby spent the next few days in her store readying it for the grand opening tonight. She tried to ignore that more than sex had happened between her and Hayden. They were both busy with work but Hayden made time for her in his schedule. He'd shown up unexpectedly one afternoon after one of her staffers had to go home for a family emergency and helped her unbox the merchandise.

He'd also taken her for a ride on his prized custom West Coast Chopper. He was everything she wanted in a man and more, and she knew she was falling hard for him. Every day revealed another facet of the man and she had yet to see anything she didn't like.

But she remembered Alan and what had brought her to Vegas and worried over that. Not to mention what she'd been forced to realize about herself that night in the private garden. That Hayden already owned her heart and soul. She could try to pretend she hadn't completely given him her heart but she knew that wasn't true.

A part of her rejoiced. After all, she'd returned to Vegas with just that goal in mind. But the other part of her worried. Alan had been out of touch since the night she and Hayden had spent on his yacht, and Shelby worried that Alan was going to show up before she had a chance to talk to Hayden.

She'd tried several times with Hayden to bring up the subject of her return to Vegas. Tried to find the words to make him understand that she hadn't realized how much he'd changed, how much she had. But last night a letter from her mom had arrived and she'd been unable to deal with anything but that.

Hayden had taken her up to his penthouse and they'd sat on his balcony and talked until two in the morning. Talked about their single parents. She'd learned more about Alan than she'd expected to. Realized that once Hayden's mom died when Hayden was quite young, Alan had focused on Hayden, making his son's success the purpose of his life outside the casino.

When Shelby had talked about her own mother, she'd realized that it wasn't her mother she was ashamed of. It was the way other people had always looked at them. She told Hayden about how her mother loved to crank up old Elvis Presley albums after dinner and they'd danced and sung while they'd cleaned the dishes.

She'd forgotten how much she'd loved her mom until that moment. She'd made the decision to call her and set up a time to visit only to have to leave a message on the answering machine when she followed through.

Shelby felt as if all the loose ends in her life were finally being straightened out. She was thirty-two and just starting to get it together.

Last night Hayden had pushed her hard to move in with him, even going so far as inviting his friends Kylie and Deacon Prescott to his penthouse for dinner. Shelby had enjoyed meeting the couple. But more than that she'd enjoyed the feeling that she and Hayden were a couple. A real couple. A happily-ever-after couple.

And that scared her.

She glanced at her watch. 8:50 a.m. She had ten minutes until she'd be addressing her staff. Paige was due in this afternoon and they were having a soft opening by invitation only for the other casino owners in the area and VIPs from each of the surrounding resorts.

A soft opening was a pre-grand opening that was a test run for business owners. Shelby was always nervous at this stage. But as she stood in her office and glanced into the showroom at the gilded shelves filled with unique, sexy lingerie, she felt her confidence return. After all, this was the twentieth store she'd opened.

Her staff had been handpicked and Shelby knew they'd do a fabulous job. She'd decided that tonight, after the formal grand opening, she'd tell Hayden she'd move in with him. And she vowed to talk to him about his dad. To let him know that Alan had blackmailed her into coming back.

She had chosen her clothing for the day carefully, donning the red leather bustier and thong under a long-camel colored suede skirt with a black silk shirt. She'd pulled her hair up into a loose chignon and left several tendrils of curls hanging around her face.

She wore a pair of black heels, and a small gold choker as her only jewelry aside from her watch. Her clothes looked good on her and gave her an added boost of confidence as she exited her office and entered the shop.

Her small staff was already assembled, talking quietly among themselves. Shelby's cell phone rang.

She glanced at the number and saw that it was Hayden. "Hey."

"Hey, yourself. Will you have time before the opening for a drink with me?"

The day was jam-packed with activities and last-minute details. "Sorry, I don't think so. I'll probably be going over something with Paige."

"How about if I come to you?" he asked.

Nothing would make her happier. She liked that Hayden had made sure his schedule was always available to her so that she could find him whenever she wanted him. "Sure. In fact, I have a little surprise for you."

"Yeah? Is it something I've been waiting for?"

She thought about it. Thought about how long they'd both been together and apart. Thought about their lives and how they'd both used work as a substitute for relationships. And thought about how this time she wasn't leaving. "Oh, yeah."

"Dammit, I'm on my way to a meeting but I want to

come to you. Take you away from all this and just make love to you."

"Stop it. We both have work to do."

"I know. I'll be by around five."

She hung up quietly and turned to her staff. After giving them a pep talk, she walked outside the shop to observe the store, to see it from beyond the gilded gold leaf–inset doors. The window displays looked erotic and sophisticated.

"Nice job."

Shelby froze. Slowly she turned to face an older, more jaded-looking version of Hayden. "What are you doing here?"

"Checking on my investment," Alan MacKenzie said, putting his hand under her elbow and leading her out of the path of the foot traffic.

Shelby took a deep breath and tried to tamp down the sense of panic she felt. Everything was starting to go so well for her and Hayden. "This really isn't a good time. You know this entire casino is wired with security cameras that record everything. I don't want Hayden to get the wrong idea."

"I don't trust you to carry out our plan," he said.

"It's not our plan," she said, pulling her arm away. "Not anymore. I'm not sure I can do what you wanted me to. Please, Alan, just leave this to me."

Shelby turned away determined to leave Alan standing there. She ran into a solid chest and glanced up with a sense of dread in the pit of her stomach.

"Hayden—"

"Leave her alone, Dad," Hayden said, putting his arm around her shoulder and anchoring her to his side. "She's here because of business, not to be bullied by you."

Shelby was shaking and she knew that this moment was going to end badly. She should have told Hayden about his dad's proposition before now. Why hadn't she?

Because she'd wanted to make sure he really liked her before she dropped her bomb. Because she'd always understood that they had to have more than a great sexual bond between them. Because she knew that she needed Hayden's love and wasn't sure she'd had enough time to convince him that what they had would last.

"I'm not bothering her, Hay. I was congratulating her on her store. She's come a long way from the girl we both knew."

"Don't say it like that, Dad. We never gave her a chance."

Hearing Hayden defend her convinced Shelby without a doubt that she couldn't put off the truth any longer. She had to tell him. But she didn't want to spoil this moment. In her entire life, she'd never had anyone defend her the way Hayden was now.

Emotion choked her and she turned her face into his chest, hugging him tightly, trying to tell him without words just what that meant to her.

Hayden was glad he'd gotten down to Bêcheur d'Or as quickly as he had. He'd been in the middle of a meeting when Deacon had called him to say that he'd spotted Alan in the casino. Alan usually visited only twice a year and always caused some sort of trouble with the staff. Last fall Alan had handed out demerit cards to half of Hayden's blackjack dealers for minor infractions, causing distress before Hayden could explain that his father had no power over casino employees.

As soon as his dad disappeared around the corner, Shelby took a few steps away from Hayden. She was pale. He'd never seen her look like this.

"Are you okay?" he asked, lifting her face toward his. There were tears in her eyes, and no matter what she said, he knew his dad had been bullying her.

She blinked and her vulnerability slowly disappeared. "It really wasn't bad. I just know what your father thinks of me. And he makes me feel like...like I'm still a gold digger."

He lowered his head for a kiss, tenderly tasting her mouth, showing without words what she meant to him. He pulled back before he wanted to because he knew she had a busy day. "Well, I know how my old man can be."

Hayden rubbed the back of his neck, not sure how to explain to her about the man he'd become after she'd left. "He blames you for a lot of things, Shelby."

"What does he blame me for?" she asked. She'd put a foot of space between them and had her arms wrapped around her waist.

"Not having grandkids."

"I doubt you've been celibate since I've been gone. There was opportunity, right?"

"I'm not much on settling down. This business is my life. Could you imagine raising a kid here? I mean you've seen the kids at the center. What kind of life is that?" he asked, not sure he wanted her to say no.

"The one you had. You turned out okay."

"I'm a workaholic adrenaline junkie."

"Thought about this a lot?"

"Nah, one of the women I dated called me that."

"She was probably jealous."

"Of what?"

"Of this casino. She probably had just figured out that no woman could come between you and the Chimera. Anyway, your dad raised you here. And you two are still on speaking terms, so it can't have been that bad."

Normally he'd never have left his steering-committee meeting like he had, but here he was several floors away from some very highly paid men and women who were waiting for him. Especially since the dressing rooms of the revue venue had been broken into last night and a nasty note had been left for his star performer.

"No, it wasn't. We get along okay when he minds his own damn business. He thinks he can stroll into my operation whenever he wants and give me tips. The old man still thinks casinos should be run…old school."

Shelby laughed like he wanted her to. He reached out to toy with one of the loose waves hanging around her face. "He has the belief that he's always right, too. He can't believe that people can change."

"People or you?"

"Me," she said, sounding forlorn.

No matter what he said or did, their past would always be between them like an unacknowledged wound.

The past hadn't been healed by years of separation nor was the relationship they were building enough to wipe away the past hurt. He really stunk at relationships and had no idea how to make this right.

The only time he really felt in control around Shelby was when she was in his arms. He walked around behind her and surrounded her with his body, pulling her back against him, wrapping his arms around her waist and bending his head to whisper in her ear. "Don't worry, baby. I'll run interference for you."

And he meant it. The last time, he'd left Shelby on her own to deal with his dad, but now he realized he should have protected her better.

Why hadn't he been able to see that she needed him? He hadn't wanted to acknowledge that they were dependent on each other.

Her hands crept up over his wrists, holding him as he held her. She tipped her head back and looked up at him. He could tell she was searching for something in his gaze and he hoped she'd find it. Frankly, he knew that taking her to bed would go a long way to making him feel better.

"I don't need protecting. I'm a grown woman."

He waggled his eyebrows at her, trying to lighten the tension that lingered in the air like a streak of bad luck at a slot machine. "I've noticed."

"Trust you to turn this back to sex."

"Did I?"

She raised both eyebrows and gave him a very prim look. "You know you did."

He winked at her. "Can't help myself around you."

She sighed and then moved away. "Thanks for coming to the rescue, but I need to get back to work."

"You're welcome. What were you doing out here?"

"Checking out the store from the outside."

"You've checked it out before," he said.

She walked toward her lingerie store and stood out of the foot traffic, watching the action inside. "Sometimes it's hard to believe it's really mine. That this is my life."

"You've worked hard for your success. You deserve it."

"I don't know about deserving all this."

She gestured to her clothing and the shop and him. "I mean, I'm wearing a pair of shoes that cost three hundred dollars. When I was in Vegas before, I bought my shoes from the final-markdown rack."

"I never knew that," he said.

"I would have died if you had. I tried very hard to hide that part of my life from you. The house you picked me up at wasn't really mine—it was the Jenkinses'. I worked there as an after-school maid. Their daughter was two years older than me and Mrs. Jenkins used to give me her old clothes."

He saw now how little he'd known of her real life. Shelby had always looked like a million bucks. He remembered how careful she was of her clothing and shoes. He'd taken it for vanity and appreciated it because she'd made him look good. But now he was beginning to realize that she may have spent all her money on looking good for him. And he'd never noticed.

He told himself he was noticing now, but in his gut he hoped it wasn't too little too late.

Paige closed the door and locked it after the last employee left. Paige was tall, almost six feet, and she wore her jet-black hair in a classic bob. She was reed thin and could have made a fortune as a model in New York if she'd wanted to. Shelby finished cleaning up and stacked champagne glasses on the counter for the catering service.

"I think Vegas likes us," Shelby said. Her entire body was humming with energy. Excitement from the opening warred with sexual anticipation.

"Someone in Vegas certainly likes you," Paige said, pointing to the very large arrangement of exotic flowers that had arrived in the middle of the afternoon.

"I hope so," she said. Paige knew her like no one else, but there were still parts of her life that she'd never shared with her friend.

"I like Hayden, too. I'm glad you decided to come back here and face him."

"Me, too. But I still haven't told him about Alan."

"When are you going to?"

"Tonight."

"Good. You deserve some happiness. Where are you going to stay now that the shop is open?"

"Depends on how things go with Hayden. I'll definitely be at the hotel for the next few weeks."

"Are you moving out here permanently?" she asked. "What about D.C.? You know I don't do openings."

"Chill out. I want to think about telecommuting. I want to give this relationship with Hayden a real chance at working. I'll still do the openings and the traveling."

Paige wrapped her arm around Shelby's waist, hugging her close. "I hate change."

"I know. But nothing is really changing."

"Yes, it is."

"I don't have to stay."

"This is the man you always bring up when we talk seriously about life. I think you better stay. Maybe we can relocate headquarters out here. There's nothing holding us to Atlanta."

"What about Palmer?" Paige's current lover was in the process of getting a divorce.

"He's going back to his wife."

"Oh, Paige. I thought they were over."

"Apparently you and I were the only ones who believed that."

"If you'd seriously consider relocating the business, I think I'd like to be here even if things with Hayden don't work out. You know, since most of our shops are back East, maybe we need a few more out West. I've been thinking of scouting Arizona."

"Like maybe Phoenix?"

"Yes, and the surrounding area," Shelby said, careful not to say more. She'd kept her mom private from Paige, never mentioning Terri Paxton to her partner and best friend.

"We'd have to research the demographics, but why not?"

"Thanks, Paige."

"For what?"

"For making me go into business with you." Shelby hugged her friend.

Paige laughed in that loud way she had. "Hey, I didn't do that. I merely pointed out that the smart thing to do was to work with me."

But they both knew that she had. Shelby pulled away from her friend and started shutting off the lights. "What are your plans for tonight?"

"Uh, hello, it's after midnight, I'm going to bed."

"But you're in Vegas. The city never sleeps."

"Maybe, but I'm a small-town girl and I need some rest. What about you?"

"I'm meeting Hayden in the casino."

They set the alarm and left the shop. Despite the fact that all the stores in the retail section closed at midnight, there was still some foot traffic, but it was lighter than it had been earlier. When they left the shopping wing and entered the main casino floor, Paige said goodnight and went up to her room.

Shelby hesitated, glancing through the crowded casino trying to find Hayden. People stood two and three deep at the slot machines and there wasn't an empty seat at the blackjack tables. Rodney the dealer smiled at her as she walked past his table.

"Have you seen Hayden?"

"There was an emergency at the revue. Some kind of security issue," Rodney said.

Shelby headed that way, feeling like she was in a

maze. No matter which direction she turned there were more people and she was starting to feel closed in.

She retreated to a quiet corner of the casino, near one of the exits. She wasn't going to find him in this throng. She'd go back to his penthouse and wait for him.

That idea appealed to her. As she walked to the elevator, the scenario she wanted to create formed in her mind. Hayden had given her so much today. More than he could ever understand. She'd felt accepted and it had been a really long time—maybe her entire life—since that had happened.

Sure, Paige accepted her but that was more from an I-know-your-dirt-and-you-know-mine aspect. Hayden accepted her on a personal level, in a way that made her feel as if she was special to him.

An arm snaked around her waist and she glanced up to meet Hayden's intense gaze. "Hey, baby. How was the opening? I'm sorry I couldn't stay, but we had a major emergency."

"What happened?" she asked. Hayden was tense.

"Roxy was attacked."

"What? By whom?"

"Some crazed fan. He cut her in several places, some deep. They took her to the emergency room and she's having surgery now. Police have the man in custody."

"Oh my God. What can I do?"

"I've got to head back to the hospital."

"I'll go with you."

"You don't have to."

"Hayden, this is what being together is about."

"Thanks," he said.

"No problem."

Ten minutes later they were seated in the hospital waiting room. About five other cast members were there as well. After an hour had passed, they decided to go to the cafeteria to get coffee. Shelby sat next to Hayden, unsure how to help him. She knew that he thought of the Chimera staff as his family and he was taking this hard.

He rubbed the bridge of his nose. "Talk to me, Shel. Tell me about your opening."

She sipped the cafeteria coffee, trying to remember the opening. It seemed as if it was years ago instead of just hours. "It went really well. I can't believe how many people showed up."

"Did Deacon come?"

"Yes, with Kylie. She invited me to have lunch with her."

"Good. I like Kylie."

"Me, too," Shelby said. And it was the truth, though she knew she had little in common with Kylie who had confessed that she'd grown up with her nose stuck in a book. Still, she'd been open and friendly and had said she was glad to see Hayden dating someone with an IQ bigger than her bra size.

Kylie had given Shelby a glimpse of what Hayden's life had become. She'd promised to tell Shelby over lunch all about the infamous bet that Hayden and Deacon had made about Kylie.

Hayden's friendship with the Prescotts was obviously a strong one. Deacon had worked the room and Kylie had hung back, quietly confessing that she wasn't the outgoing person her husband was. She'd also told Shelby not to let being a casino owner's wife intimidate her. But Shelby knew whatever happened in Vegas, Hayden wouldn't ask her to marry him again.

The man in question spoke again, snapping her out of her thoughts. "Did you check out of my hotel?"

"Yes, earlier. I…well, darn, I was hoping to keep that a secret from you."

"Why? Did my dad bother you again? I told him to back off."

"No, nothing like that. I kind of had a surprise for you. But it doesn't seem right to bring it up now."

He put his arm around her and hugged her to his side. "We can have your surprise tomorrow. Tonight I need you to stay with me, baby. I'm trying to go slow and not pressure you, but…will you stay, please?"

Tears burned the back of her eyes and any doubts that she had about staying in Vegas totally disappeared. There was something between her and Hayden that couldn't be denied. And they both knew it.

Reaching up, she cupped his jaw in her hands. "That was my surprise. I'm not leaving your hotel. I'm just moving out of my room and up to your place."

His eyes narrowed. "For tonight?"

"And longer. If you still want me."

He pulled her to him, his mouth finding hers. His hands roamed up and down her back, forcing her more fully against him.

She clutched his shoulders, letting him support her

entire body. Someone at an adjacent table cleared his throat and Hayden lifted his head. But he didn't glance away from her.

She fingered her mouth where her lips still throbbed from his kiss. "I guess that means yes?"

Nine

Hayden couldn't believe the way everything was falling together. Shelby was moving in with him and now Roxy's doctor was giving him a positive report. Roxy had come through her surgery and was resting comfortably. She'd be able to return home in a few days.

Hayden knew Roxy had no family. He'd met her when she was sixteen. A runaway who was out of options wherever she'd come from; he'd never asked. He'd given her a job in one of the restaurants and a place to sleep. The rest, as they say, was history.

He talked to Roxy's doctor and to some of the other cast members of the revue who had agreed to stay with her overnight.

Hayden walked down the brightly lit hospital hallway to see Shelby standing there waiting for him. It seemed almost too easy that she was moving into his penthouse now. God knew that convincing Shelby had been harder than he'd expected.

But there was something right about it happening now. Something right about having her back with him after all this time. Something in his soul said that this hand was playing out accordingly and he should just keep playing the winning cards dealt him.

She slipped her arm around his waist. "Is she okay?"

He nodded. "Let's get out of here."

They were back at the hotel a few minutes later. The lobby was still a beehive of activity even though it was almost three in the morning. Hayden wanted to go up to his penthouse with Shelby but he had to make one more swing through the casino and check in with security.

"Babe."

She arched one eyebrow at him. "Yes?"

"I've got about thirty minutes' worth of work left tonight."

She nodded toward a comfortable-looking chair. "I'll wait over there for you."

Hayden conducted his meetings as quickly as possible and returned to Shelby.

"Where's your luggage?" he asked.

"I brought it up to your place earlier. Was that okay?"

She kept asking him as if she was afraid he'd changed his mind. "Of course. I gave you a key the first night you came back into my life."

She shrugged. "There's a part of me that's afraid to trust this, Hayden. The last time things moved so quickly."

"And they are again. But you have to face the fact that you and I live life at this speed. You wouldn't be able to wait months for me. Any more than I can wait that long for you."

She nibbled on her lower lip as they waited for the elevator and he tightened his arm around her waist. He wanted to stake his claim for the world to see. Yet at the same time he knew he wanted to take his time with her. To make sure that she understood how her action this night had impacted him.

He needed her in ways she couldn't understand. This wasn't the first time one of his employees had been injured on the job. But tonight with Shelby by his side... she soothed him. She gave him someone to share his burden with and he wanted to say thank-you to her without having to actually utter the words.

He shivered a little at the thought. She was the only woman he'd ever let in to his soul. He'd never been able to keep her out—then or now.

The elevator doors opened and they stepped onto the public car. There were two other couples and Shelby chatted to them as they rode to the fifth floor where they'd change cars. When they exited, she wished them both luck and slipped her hand into Hayden's.

"You'll make a good casino owner's wife," he said.

The words slipped out without intent.

"Hayden—"

He bent, taking her mouth with his. He didn't want

her to think or explain. He knew it was too soon, but knowing didn't stop him from wanting. And he wanted Shelby. She was what he craved deep in his soul, and he knew he was going to do whatever it took to make her agree to marry him.

He lifted his head. "Let's go home so I can make love to you."

She nodded and was quiet until they reached his front door. Then she stopped, grasping his wrists and holding each one in one of her small delicate hands. Her hands didn't even wrap completely around his wrist.

"Are you sure about this?"

"About what?" he asked, his mind already on the way she'd feel under his body. To finally make love to her in his bed was a fantasy he'd been entertaining for too long now.

"Me and you," she said.

He brought her hand to his body, where he was already hardening, readying to take this one woman who had always been so elusive. "This answer your question?"

She shook her head. "Not that. About me living with you. There's still so much about me you don't know." She *had* to talk to him about Alan. But…not now.

"I know the important stuff."

"This?" she asked, her fingers caressing him.

"Well, yeah, but more than that. I know that you grew up without any luxuries and that you don't like to take money or gifts from others. That you work hard to make your dreams come true but never at the expense of others."

He swept her up in his arms, bending to unlock the door and open it. He entered his apartment, then kicked the door closed behind him.

"I know that I need you in a way I never wanted to need any woman. That when I kiss you, you go up like fire in my arms."

He walked straight through the public rooms of his home, past the poker table and the doors leading to the balcony where he'd had breakfast with her. He entered his bedroom. One entire wall was floor-to-ceiling windows that looked out on his kingdom. His world. Vegas. The 24/7 lifestyle he'd always thrived on.

It paled in comparison with the lovely woman in his arms. He hugged her closer to him, buried his face in the curls at her nape. He inhaled her scent deep into him. Deep into his soul.

"I know that I want you here always. I want to keep you in my bed waiting for me. Ready to make love to every second of every day."

She lifted her head from his shoulders, her hands encircling his neck and her mouth finding his. She kissed him deeply and every part of his being responded. His erection strained against his pants. His chest swelled, his blood flowing heavier in his veins.

"I want that, too. But I couldn't bear it if you had regrets," she said softly.

He let her slide down his body, his hands settling on her hips when she would have moved away. "How could I regret the biggest win of my lifetime?"

* * *

Shelby knew in this moment she'd made the right choice. That all the pain of the past was fading away as she stood next to Hayden in his bedroom. Hayden was a good man with a deep well of caring inside him.

"I'm not good at taking chances," she said. "I worried about your reaction to my moving in here. But no more. Sit on the bed." The bed, she noticed now, was huge, the prominent feature in the dark-walled room appointed sparsely with sleek Danish furniture.

He raised one eyebrow at her. "I don't want to wait."

"Yes, you do. Trust me."

He settled onto the bed, leaning back on his elbows and watching her through narrowed eyes. "Okay."

Even in supposedly ceding control to her, power still radiated from him.

Once he was there watching her, nerves assailed her.

"Shelby, come here."

When she crossed to him, Hayden sat up, widening his legs and drawing her between them. "What's going on in that head of yours?"

She hated that she'd messed this up. "I wanted to give you your fantasy."

"You already have."

"No, something sexy but…"

He raised both eyebrows and brought his hands to the buttons on her shirt. Slowly he opened them, revealing the curves of her breasts where they swelled over the top of a bustier.

He leaned down and kissed the pale white globes.

Her breasts felt fuller under his lips. Holding the sides of her blouse in either hand, he drew the fabric across her skin, rubbing all over her but keeping that layer of material between her and his hands.

The torture was exquisite and she arched her back, tried to move his touch where she needed it. But he controlled her carefully, finally removing her blouse and tossing it on the floor.

He didn't take his eyes from her breasts, and watching him gave her the confidence she'd been lacking. She straightened her shoulders and ran her hands up her thighs to her waist, cinched in by the bustier.

He leaned back on his elbows and watched her. She took a half step away from him, to give herself some more room. She twirled around, feeling the suede skirt slide around her legs.

All day she'd been hyperaware of what she wore under her clothes. Aware that Hayden's eyes would glaze, just as they were doing now, when he realized what she wore. At this moment she knew she'd never been more perfect. More the perfect woman for Hayden, the perfect mate for him. The perfect person she'd always been so afraid of being.

Remembering what Hayden had said when he'd first seen her dressing the mannequin, she unfastened the skirt and partially unzipped it, letting it fall to her hips. She swayed them in time to the music that had been playing in the casino earlier. The slow steady beat of the Marsalis jazz that Hayden loved.

She danced around the room for him. Lost all track

of her body and the imagined flaws she didn't want him to see. Lost complete track of her fears that Alan would somehow ruin what she'd found with Hayden. Lost all of her inhibitions. She offered her body up to Hayden in a slow, sensual dance.

Hayden pushed to his feet. Slowly he unbuttoned his shirt, moving his body in the same rhythm as hers. He danced behind her, his hands coming to her hips and pushing the zipper the rest of the way down. He pulled her back against his erection as he moved with her, each undulation of their bodies inflaming them both a little more.

Her skirt fell farther, stopping just above her knees. She spread her legs, rubbed her backside against Hayden.

He groaned low in his throat, his hands afire on her body as he swept them up and down her torso. He cupped her breasts and pressed hot, wet kisses to her neck and shoulder blades.

Still the music burned inside of her, building to a crescendo in time with the desire flowing through her body. She turned in his arms, pushing his shirt to the floor, fumbling with his belt buckle, finally freeing it. He caught her up in his arms, carrying her the few short feet to the bed.

Tossing her onto the surface, he followed her down, one knee between her legs to keep them open. His hands on either side of her shoulders, he braced himself above her and slowly lowered his chest to hers. His mouth teased hers as his fingers and hands tormented her breasts. He found the pull-away cups on the bustier and ripped them off. He bent to her, suckling her into his mouth with deep, strong tugs of his lips.

Shelby shifted her hips on the bed. Needing more. Needing it now. Not it, him. She needed him deep inside her. She wanted to share with him this feeling that swamped her and made her want to be what he'd said earlier. Want to be worthy of his love.

He pushed her skirt and thong down her legs and freed himself. He fumbled in the nightstand for a box of condoms. She took it from him and opened it carefully.

She took his length in her hand, sliding up and down a few times before she placed the condom on its tip and smoothed it down his erection.

Groaning, he gripped her hips, pushing one pillow and then a second under them, angling her up for his penetration. He held her hips in his hands and stared into her eyes. She met his gaze as he brought himself to the entrance of her body.

"You're mine," he said, thrusting deep inside her.

He set a pace that drove them quickly toward the pinnacle. "Say it, baby. Say that you're mine."

She gasped for breath, felt everything shimmering so close to her. Her orgasm hovered just out of reach. She met his gaze and realized what she'd been waiting for.

"I'm yours, Hayden. Only yours."

They both tumbled over the edge. Hayden's voice echoed in the room as he shouted her name. Shelby clutched him close, realizing that something had changed in the foundation of their relationship and that there was no going back.

* * *

Hayden woke up twice in the night, assured himself that Shelby was still in his bed and made love to her. He was ravenous for her body. He couldn't get enough of the way she reacted to his every touch.

He rolled to his side, propped himself up on his elbow and stared down at the woman who'd haunted him since he'd first met her. Back then he'd been way too young to appreciate her, but there'd always been something about Shelby that quieted his soul and gave him the peace he longed for.

The sheet was bunched around her waist. She lay on her side with her arms curved under her breasts. His morning erection swelled. God, he'd never been this insatiable before.

The alarm buzzed before he could touch her. He shut it off. She smiled sleepily up at him and he felt a sense of rightness with his world that he'd seldom experienced before. Leaning down, he kissed her. She pulled back.

"I'm sore," she said softly, blushing.

He ran his hands down her body, hoping to soothe her aches. "I'm sorry."

"Don't be. I just can't this morning," she said, leaning up to kiss his whiskered jaw. She rubbed her hands over his face and down his chest. "I missed you."

"When?" He hadn't left her side the entire night.

"When I left."

He knew she was referring to their time together ten years ago. "I was so angry."

"I know. That's why I waited until I was at the airport to call."

"Why'd you do it?"

"The money."

"And no trust in me to provide it."

He rolled to his side. He hadn't meant to rehash the past but it seemed inevitable. Neither of them had ever really had their say.

He felt her move behind him, the bed dipping slightly beneath her weight as her arm snaked around his waist. She held him to her, her face buried between his shoulder blades. She brushed a soft kiss on his back.

"I…I needed the money. I'd spent my entire life believing that money would solve my problems. Remember how I told you I didn't grow up in that house you picked me up at?"

Her hand fluttered on his stomach, not caressing but gesturing nervously, trying to explain without saying the necessary words.

He realized anew how much he cared for this woman, and how little he'd known of her before. He rolled over, needing to face her. To see what she was feeling as she spoke. She wouldn't look at him. She dipped her head, tucking her face between his neck and shoulder. "Where did you live?"

She took a deep breath; he felt the warmth of her exhalation against his skin. His body stirred despite the fact that now wasn't the time. He closed his eyes and fought for control.

"In that dumpy trailer park four miles from town, the Silver Horseshoe."

He shuddered. He knew the place. Full of degenerates, drug dealers, prostitutes and other unsavory characters. How could Shelby have grown up there? She was worlds too soft for that kind of life.

"You know it?" she asked when he didn't respond.

"Yeah, baby, I do." Rubbing his hands down her back, he wanted to pull her completely into his body. To vow to protect her from everything, even the dark memories of her past.

He held her, rocking her gently to give her some comfort. He sensed she wasn't really here with him but had traveled back to that place she'd grown up in.

"When your dad offered me a million, I just couldn't take a chance that it might never come again. I couldn't go back to that place. Plus, he threatened to tell you about where I came from. And I knew he was going to cut you off and once you knew I'd lied about who I was… Well, I'm not the gambler you are. I had to take the sure thing."

He heard the conviction in her voice and understood for the first time what it must have taken for her to leave him. To be honest, every time she'd broached the subject of how they'd live without his dad's money, he'd put her off. He knew that he had funds the old man couldn't touch but he'd never shared that knowledge with her. And now he saw that he should have. That maybe he hadn't trusted her the way she'd needed him to.

"God, baby. I'm sorry." He bent his head and rested

his chin on her shoulder. The silky length of her hair fell on his shoulders and he just held her in his arms. She was all that was delicate and feminine. She had always had to protect herself, even once he'd come into her life. He wished he could go back in time and kick his own ass for never seeing beyond her body.

She lifted her face and there were tears pooling in her eyes, but she blinked to keep them from falling. "Don't be. I used you. I knew you had money from the first time you asked me out. I had to pay Christy Jenkins to take me to the country club with her. I was looking for a rich guy and I found you."

He was a little angry to hear her say so bluntly what she'd done. But he'd picked her for precisely the same reason. Because his dad wouldn't like her. He knew that he could screw this up again. That the last piece of the puzzle that was Shelby had yet to be revealed. But he also knew that this woman belonged to him. And if it took a lifetime to figure her out, that was fine by him. He fought to find the right things to say. And knew he'd fail miserably.

"I was just a bonus?" he asked, attempting some levity where there was none. He hated that she made him vulnerable but she did. Because even back then her loss had hurt him more deeply than he'd ever admitted to himself.

He waited for her to answer, wishing he'd kept his mouth shut or just gotten out of bed before their conversation had come to this point.

"No. You were more. I can't explain it but from the beginning I knew you'd break my heart."

Ten

The next week flew by. Hayden and Shelby visited Roxy in the hospital. But the showgirl wasn't always up for company. They went every day anyway. Shelby reminded Hayden a bit of Roxy. Both women had come from nothing to make great successes of their lives.

Each day Shelby's life and his become more seamlessly wrapped together. It didn't matter that Hayden's schedule was hectic. He made time for her in between meetings with the incoming television-poker people, visits to the kids' facility and other casino details.

Shelby, too, was busy with training a manager for her store and phone meetings with the developers of the D.C. project.

Tonight was one of their rare free nights, and they'd

chosen to spend it with the Prescotts, at the penthouse, for dinner and a game of poker.

Shelby sat across the small card table from him. Deacon and Kylie were on either side of them. The room smelled of cigars and fajitas. He had a hard time even calling this a real poker game. The women, having not spent the last fifteen years of their lives living in a casino, didn't have the same experience at the game that he and Deacon did.

By unspoken agreement the men were playing to the women's level.

He glanced up at Shelby and caught her staring at him. She flushed, so he knew the direction of her thoughts. He raised one eyebrow.

Deacon cleared his throat. "I believe it's your turn, Mac."

Damn. How had this happened? He had been determined to claim Shelby again—not to be captured by her. She had always been a fire in his soul and now that she was here and his, it was worse. Some nights he woke and stared down at her sleeping face just to make sure she was really here.

And that pissed him off. He was a cool player. A man of confidence. Not a person easily shook. But she shook him.

He glanced at his hand and tossed two cards on the table. "I'll take two."

Deacon gave him two cards. Hayden picked them up, realizing he had a full house. A pair of aces and three tens. A full house… That echoed in his mind. He'd been a loner for so long, but now he was living with someone. Not just anyone. Shelby.

Could he ever stand at the end of the aisle waiting for her again? He wanted her to stay with him.

She'd rounded out his life, showed him things that had been missing before. She loved every aspect of his life, even gambling, which she was horrible at. He'd never met a person with worse luck at cards than she had.

Kylie's green eyes twinkled as she took one card. Shelby grimaced at her hand. "How many do I have to keep?"

"Two," Hayden said.

She tossed three cards on the table. Deacon gave her three new ones. Deacon sorted his hand out and they all played to see Hayden's hand. Shelby should have folded.

"Baby, you don't have to stay in when your hand is that bad."

"I was bluffing."

Kylie laughed kindly, and brushed back her long brown hair. "Not very well. I'm not good at this either. Deacon has been giving me tips."

Hayden glanced over at his friend and saw him shrug. "What can I say? She thinks I'm an expert at everything."

Kylie scoffed. "Hardly. But you have potential."

"Can you believe the way she treats me? Not married two years and already she's seeing the tarnish on my armor."

Kylie smiled at her husband, reached across the table to take his hand. He rubbed the back of her knuckles with his thumb. "You're still my hero," she said, smiling into his eyes.

Shelby glanced at Hayden and then pushed her chair back. "I think I'll clean up these plates."

Hayden grabbed a couple of plates and followed her into the kitchen.

"I like your friends," she said.

"Yeah?"

"Yeah. They seem so…perfect for each other. How'd they meet?"

"Deacon saw her on a security monitor and said she was the one for him. I bet him he couldn't convince her to marry him, so he went down and found her and asked her out."

She punched his arm. "What were you thinking?"

He rubbed his arm. "Hey, it worked out okay."

"I guess. But why would you do that?"

"Relationships don't make sense to me. Gambling always does. I knew that Deacon wanted her but I wasn't sure he'd really go after her."

"So you gave him a nudge."

He shrugged, and crossing to the sink, he dropped the plates into the sink. Shelby moved around him, cleaning up the remains of their dinner dishes and putting them all in the dishwasher.

Hayden leaned against the countertop and watched her. There was something right about this and he wished there was some way he could not screw this up. But he'd spoken the truth to Shelby. He didn't understand relationships.

The kitchen door opened and Deacon and Kylie

poked their heads in. "We're going to take off. Thanks for the game and dinner."

"You're welcome," Hayden said. Shelby dried her hands and came to stand next to him. He slipped his arm around her waist and together they walked Kylie and Deacon out of the penthouse.

Hayden didn't hear anything they said as they left. He wasn't aware of anything but the feel of Shelby under his arm. When the door closed, he backed her up against it.

He swallowed her gasp of surprise with his mouth. She wrapped her arms around his shoulders and held on to him, let him control the kiss and the embrace. He slid his leg between hers and bent his knee.

He swept his hands down her body, cupping her rump and pulling her lower body into his. She straddled his leg, her hands clinging to his shoulders.

She pulled back to breathe. "What was that for?"

"For being you."

He swept her up in his arms and carried her into the bedroom and made love to her through the night. He hoped it would be enough of a bond to hold her to him for all time.

Shelby sank back into her leather office chair. Everything she'd ever wanted was within her grasp. The new store was more successful than she'd dreamed possible. But then Shelby had remembered the Vegas of her youth, not this new vibrant scene with too much money and elegance.

Hayden was gone for the day, flying some high rollers who had been staying at his hotel every year since he'd opened out over the Grand Canyon in Deacon's helicopter. Shelby had gone to Roxy's house earlier to drop off some flowers for her.

It made no sense in the factual world but Shelby swore she could feel that Hayden wasn't in the hotel and she missed him.

"Ms. Paxton, there's a guy out front asking for you," said one of her staffers, sticking her head into Shelby's office.

"Thanks. Tell him I'll be right there."

Shelby stood and straightened her suit. She'd had five different men seek her out and ask her to personally select an intimate wardrobe for their wives, girlfriends or mistresses. The service was one that Paige and she had offered from the beginning, but usually it wasn't that popular.

She smiled as she exited her office, but froze when she saw that it was Alan MacKenzie. God knew he wasn't here for her professional help.

Her staff was helping a guest near the fitting rooms and Stan, their stock-boy-turned-salesperson, was flirting with a couple of women in their early twenties.

"How can I help you?" she asked Alan. Hayden looked a lot like his father, except in the eyes.

"We didn't get to finish our conversation the other day."

"Come into my office," she said, pivoting on her heel and leading the way. She knew she needed to resolve this. If she'd told Hayden the truth weeks ago, this wouldn't be a problem now.

Alan followed her into her office and took a seat in one of the guest chairs. Shelby went around behind the desk and seated herself. She knew it was petty but she liked sitting behind her big expensive executive's desk. Because in the back of her mind every time she saw Alan she remembered how cold, small and cheap she'd felt when she'd taken that check from him.

"I'm not your enemy here."

But he always had been. From the first time they'd been introduced, he'd always looked at her as if she wasn't good enough for his son. Even when he'd come to her in Atlanta, she'd sensed his distaste for her. Just once she wanted…what?

She knew it was impossible but she'd love to find a way to be accepted by everyone. To find that seemingly easy way that Hayden had of being everyone's equal, be it the croupier, the first-time gambler, his celebrity friends or her.

"I think we both know you never liked me," she said carefully.

"Yes, but my son always has. Why else would I be doing this?"

"I honestly don't know. Thank you for telling me about the shopping wing and suggesting that Bêcheur d'Or bid on the lease here. But that's all this is."

"I think we both know I forced you to come back."

"I would do anything for my company."

He leaned deeper into his chair, crossing his legs and staring at her. She felt the way she imagined a stripper did at that last moment when she was finally naked in front of a crowd. Shelby rubbed her hands up and down her arms.

"You came back for more than this shop and we both know it."

"No, Alan, I didn't. There's nothing more to my being here."

"I thought you were past lying like this."

Shelby flinched. "I'm not a liar."

He narrowed his eyes and Shelby wished she'd never asked him back here.

"Aren't you living with my son?" he asked.

"Yes, but—"

"Are you sleeping with him?"

She nodded. There was no way Hayden was ever going to believe she hadn't been manipulating him. No way. She heard in Alan's voice the same emotionless tone that Hayden sometimes used when he was angry.

"Mr. MacKenzie, please leave."

He pushed to his feet. "Why?"

"Because you are never going to believe I care for your son."

"Do you?"

She bit her lower lip and nodded. He'd never understand how deeply she cared for Hayden. She was sure she did. But she knew there was no way she was going to allow his father to hurt him through her again.

"That's all I needed to know."

"I'm…I'm not sure how to tell Hayden about you and me," she said. Being around Hayden had shown her the value in asking for help…asking for others' opinions. He leaned on his friends when he needed to. Right now she needed to figure out how to fix things with Hayden. And his dad…well, his dad seemed like the only one she could turn to.

"I'll handle that."

He walked out of her office and she sat there feeling shell-shocked. What was Alan going to do? Time was running out for her and Hayden. She had to tell him the truth.

Her phone rang and she hesitated to answer it. She'd been hopeful that she'd left behind that little trailer-park girl, but no matter how far she ran or how much she changed, that girl was still deep inside her.

Finally picking it up and clearing her throat, she said, "Bêcheur d'Or, where your every fantasy is made reality."

"I like the sound of that," Hayden said. His deep voice brushed over her bruised soul like a soothing balm.

"Hayden."

"What's up, baby? You okay?"

"Yes. Just having a busy day," she said. The day was going to get worse, she knew, because she had to talk to him. Not on the phone but in person. And she had to be prepared that he would see the facts and not the feelings behind her actions. "I have to fly to D.C. next week."

"How long will you be gone?"

"Three days."

"You're coming back?"

"Yes. Of course."

"Good, I'm on my way back. Meet me up front and I'll take you away from your mundane life and give you the fantasy one you deserve."

She smiled at that. Hayden was more than a fantasy.

He always knew the right things to say to make her feel better. "Okay."

When she hung up the phone, she took a deep breath. The truth was never easy, but Shelby was determined to set everything straight. Tonight.

The casino floor was buzzing with activity. Hayden was greeted by many people as he moved toward the roulette tables. Shelby's small hand was tucked into his and she followed him quietly.

There was a sadness in her eyes that he couldn't banish. Trying to prove to himself that he could be the man she needed by not taking her to bed was harder than he thought. His gut said to make love to her and get rid of the shadows that way. In bed there was no confusion or doubts between them. Just the kind of white-hot heat that burned away everything and left the two of them with their souls bared.

"The casino is busy tonight," Shelby said.

"Yeah, it is. Damn."

"What is it?"

"Someone is in the casino who shouldn't be."

"Who?"

"A grifter," Hayden said. It didn't matter that he'd known Bart since they were both four years old. Bart's family had lost everything in the early eighties and he felt that the world owed him something because of it.

"Grifter? What is that? Someone like a whale?" she asked.

Hayden didn't really want the grimier side of the casino business to touch her. He pulled her out of the foot traffic behind a row of slot machines.

"No. He's a con man. Can I leave you alone for a minute?"

"Yes, I'll be fine. I'm going to try to figure out roulette."

"Don't bet any money until I get back," he said. He felt bad taking her money. He didn't mind it when others lost in the casino, but seeing Shelby lose anything bothered him.

"Why not?" she asked, teasing him. He was glad to see her smile.

"Because I don't want your money."

"I might win."

"I doubt it!"

He kissed her quickly and walked away. He felt her watching him as he moved through the casino floor. The con man he'd seen noticed Hayden moving toward him. Bart was a regular in Vegas. A grifter who had been in and out of jail more times than anyone wanted to acknowledge.

Bart's family had lived next to Hayden's in Henderson before Hayden's mother had died. And there was a part of Hayden that wanted to help out the kid he'd known back then.

Bart gave him a salute and turned and sprinted through the crowd toward the exit. Hayden keyed his two-way phone and alerted security. He also sent a quick e-mail to the other owners, alerting them that Bart was back in town and looking for action.

He rejoined Shelby but kept scanning the crowd. "Are you ready to play?"

"I'm not sure I understand the game."

Hayden pulled her back against his body, just because he missed holding her. "Everyone is given a different colored chip to buy in so that they don't get confused. Then they place their colored chip on the number they think the ball will land on."

"This isn't very scientific, is it?" she asked after a few minutes.

From what she'd said and what he'd observed, she liked everything to fall neatly into a slot. And gambling wasn't going to do that. In fact, much of Hayden's life wasn't going to do that.

"Not at all. Every roulette player is hoping that Lady Luck will be at his side when he puts his chip on a number. In the U.S. we play with thirty-eight slots. In Europe they play on thirty-seven."

"What's the difference?"

"We have an extra zero spot."

They watched while the eight players placed their bets and the wheel spun. Hayden felt Shelby hold her breath as the ball bounced and then finally stopped.

"Oh, look, there was a winner," she said, though it wasn't she.

"Yes, and several losers."

"That's good for you."

"Yes, it is."

She was quiet again then turned in his arms, looking up at him with those big eyes of hers, their depths fathomless, guarding the secrets of her soul. "I'm not sure I'll ever understand this game well enough to play it."

"That's okay."

"No, it's not. This is your life, Hayden. I want to be a part of it."

"I don't understand everything that you do."

She wrinkled her forehead. "But you do. It's business. And you definitely understand the corporate world."

"So do you."

Hugging her closer to him for a minute, he bent his head and nibbled on her neck. "You fit right here, Shel, and that's all that matters to me."

"I'm just afraid this won't last. That after the bells and whistles fade, we won't have anything solid."

He raised both eye brows at her. "I can't do the relationship discussion thing, Shel. It's not my strong suit. Suffice it to say, we have the important things in common."

"What? And don't say sex."

"Well, we do have that," he said. He led her through the casino and then down the short hallway until they were outside. The night air was warm, wrapping around them. Hayden led her down the path toward the pool bar. "We also have business in common, and similar taste in music. And you make me laugh."

He ordered them both drinks, a sweet Bellini for Shelby and a scotch neat for him. As she perched on the bar stool, he knew there was only one thing to do. Reaching into his pocket, he fingered the ring she'd sent back to him via his father more than ten years ago.

Oh, man, was he really going to do this?

She stared out over the pool. He threw back his scotch and signaled the bartender for another one.

"Hey, Shel. I have something to ask you."

She turned to look up at him, and for a moment everything in his life felt perfect.

Eleven

Shelby took a deep breath, suddenly unsure of what was going on. She'd planned her big confession but now he wanted to ask her something. Apparently after he tipped back his second scotch in just a few minutes.

"What?" she asked. This wasn't like him. She was worried. Had his father already told him? Once again was she a pawn in the power struggle between these two MacKenzie men?

She took a sip of her favorite, sweet peach-flavored wine. It never failed to amaze her that he remembered little details about her.

"Nothing. Don't worry. Let's walk."

She'd barely tasted her drink but she left it behind. She didn't understand Hayden when he was this way.

He always moved through the world as if he owned it. To be honest, that was one of the things that drew her to him. He was always in charge, but tonight he seemed…nervous.

He tucked her under his arm, pulled her up against his body as they walked around the grounds. The moon was full and the night air warm. The scents of the flowers and night-blooming plants filled the air. The distant sounds of voices raised in revelry and assorted casino noises provided just the right background music.

Vegas was alive and the rhythm of it beat through her body in time with her heart. This was Hayden's world and she wanted to become a part of it so that they'd always be together.

"When I built this place I was full of anger, you know. I just wanted to prove to my dad and in part to you that you'd both been wrong about me."

There was no emotion in his words, just a calm telling of what had happened. As if she hadn't ripped his heart out and then coldly left him behind. For a moment, she wanted to go back in time and slap the young girl she'd been. Rationally she knew she couldn't have stayed. Knew that if she'd attempted to, their marriage would have ended in divorce. But she wished she'd found the courage to talk to him. To really show him who she'd been.

"Oh, Hayden, I'm so sorry. It was never that I doubted you." The words sounded almost too pat. They weren't enough. They didn't really explain what had been going on in her mind at the time.

"I know that now," he said, stopping under a large

magnolia tree. He pulled her into his arms, held her gently against him.

She loved the way he did that. Held her like she was precious to him. Like it mattered to him if something hurt her. She couldn't explain, but it made her feel as if she'd finally found a person with whom she could share everything.

"The Chimera is a first-rate hotel and casino." She was filled with pride every time she saw it. She remembered the run-down old hotel that had stood here before. Hayden had taken something that would have made many men bitter and turned it into not only a profitable business but also a community enhancement. He'd given back to Vegas despite the fact that the city hadn't brought him the jackpot he'd been searching for when she'd left him at the altar.

"That's right. But it's not enough anymore. For a while I've been searching for something more but I've done it all. Brought in exhibits many said no one would visit. With Deacon we've upgraded everything you can imagine, from shopping to shows to casino floors. There's nothing left for me to achieve."

He pulled away from her, rubbing the back of his neck. In the moonlight his features were stark, harsh with the emotions she knew he didn't want to reveal.

"I don't know how to say this," he said at last.

She swallowed hard and realized that the idyllic time they'd been indulging in the last few weeks was over. Hayden was a man of action and he couldn't just keep moving along without a plan.

"Say what? Do you want me to leave? Am I making you remember the anger that drove you to build this place?" she asked, wrapping her arms around herself. God, she hated feeling this way. Just once she wanted to be enough for someone. No, not anyone but Hayden. She wanted to be worthy of the kind of kingdom he'd built.

"No," he said. "Dammit, I want you to stay. Not just for a few weeks or months but forever. I want to have you in bed every night. I want to be able to call you during the day and just hear your sweet, sexy voice. I want to spend my nights laughing and loving you."

She took a deep breath. "I want that, too. More than anything. I never expected to fall in love with you again, but somehow I have."

He reached for her, pulled her to him, bending to her and kissing her fiercely. His mouth moved down her neck, pushing her shirt out of his way. He nibbled and suckled against her skin. She knew he was leaving behind a small mark, as he'd done continually since her return to Vegas, and she relished the brand.

He lifted his head and she met his gaze. There was something hot and possessive in his eyes. "Am I branded as yours?"

"Yes. But it's not enough. I want a permanent symbol of our life together. A permanent reminder to both of us that you belong to me."

"Will you have one, too?" she asked. "I don't want to be your possession."

"Yes. I…I want you to marry me, Shelby. But I can't go through the big wedding we planned last time."

She swallowed, realizing what she'd taken away from Hayden when she'd left him as she had. She hated herself for that. She bit her lip and hugged him close to her, burying her face against his chest. Not wanting him to see her own self-loathing.

"So?"

"Of course I'll marry you. There's no one I'd rather share my life with than you."

But she knew she couldn't go to a chapel one more time with secrets between them. She allowed herself this one last night of peace between them. In the morning she'd tell him the truth. Tell him about his father and the deal she'd accepted to return to Vegas and to him.

Arousal flooded his body and he had to claim her. Why the hell had he picked such a public place for this? The ring still sat in his pocket and he knew he wanted to see it on her finger.

This time it meant more than it had the last time. When he'd originally purchased the ring, he'd done so because it was the most expensive one at the jeweler's. Over the years that ring had become his talisman, his way of thumbing his nose at his father and the rest of the world.

Now it would be on her hand again and he couldn't help but feel that Shelby was his good-luck charm. That maybe she had been from the beginning.

"Let's get out of here. I want to make love to you," he said.

She nodded, slipping her small hand in his. He led

them quickly through the casino and to his private elevator. As soon as the doors closed behind them, he took her in his arms, backed her up against the rich walnut-paneled walls.

Her hands slipped to his waist, holding him to her. "Don't regret this," she said softly.

As if he could. He took her mouth with his, leaving not one inch unexplored. He caged her face in his hands, tipped her head farther back so that he could go deeper.

He vowed to brand her all over as his. Her hair wrapped around his fingers, tying them together in one more way. He lifted his head. Her eyes were closed, her face flushed, her lips wet and swollen from his kisses.

He lowered his mouth to the slim length of her neck, nibbling at her smooth flesh until he encountered her blouse.

"Bare yourself for me. Show me you want this."

Her eyes opened. "I always want you."

Her hands came between them, slowly unbuttoning her silky blouse. He followed her hands, tasting each bit of flesh as she revealed it. He lingered at her belly button and then started back up her body, stopping between her breasts, which were still covered by the ends of her shirt.

"Offer me your breasts."

She shivered; he felt the tremble that swept over her body. Her hands tightened on the edges of her blouse until her knuckles were almost white. Then carefully she pulled back the edges, revealing first the incredibly soft white skin of her breasts and then her berry-hard nipples.

The elevator bell rang, signaling their arrival at his penthouse. He lifted her in his arms. "Wrap your legs around me."

She did as he commanded and he carried her quickly to his front door and keyed it open. Once inside he went to the floor-to-ceiling windows overlooking the city of Vegas. His city and his woman. He had them both in his arms.

He took her nipple in his mouth, suckling her strongly, trying to quench a thirst that had been a part of him for so long he wasn't sure when it had started. Only that he was still thirsty for her.

Her hands roamed over his back. He wanted her hands on his skin. He set her down and ripped his shirt from his body, tossing it aside. Shelby pushed her blouse off as well. When she reached for her skirt, he stopped her.

"Just take your panties off."

She nodded, reaching under her skirt to remove them. He took a condom from his pocket and quickly sheathed himself. Then he removed the ring, holding it in his fist.

He turned Shelby in his arms, bent her forward, supporting her with his arm around her waist. "This is my life, my kingdom. It means nothing to me without you by my side."

He rubbed his erection against her hot core and she moaned, undulating against him. He skimmed his fisted hand down her body, rubbing his knuckles over her hardened nipples as he bit lightly at her nape.

He slid his hand farther down her body, brushing over the tight curls at the apex of her thighs. He felt her wetness on his fingers, on the tops of her thighs. He loved how hot she got for him.

He slipped two fingers between her legs, teasing her opening. Pushing his thigh between hers, he forced her legs open wider. He held himself poised at the entrance of her body.

"Hayden…"

"Yes?" he asked, teasing her by rubbing in small circles around her core, dipping his fingers in briefly and then pulling them out.

"What are you waiting for?"

"For you to be wearing my ring," he said, bringing his hand up her body and opening his fist.

She caught her breath. "You kept it?"

"I had to," he admitted. He took her hand and pushed the ring onto her finger. Then he brought her hand to his mouth and kissed her. The scent of her arousal was on his fingers and inflamed the lust already straining the limits of his control.

He twined their fingers together and pressed their joined hands against the plate-glass window. "I'm not letting you go."

"Good," she said.

With his free hand he positioned himself at the entrance to her body and anchoring her with his arm around her waist, he plunged deep inside her. Her body tightened around his as he continued to thrust, driving her rapidly toward first one climax and then slowly building her to another.

This time he tumbled over the edge with her. He bit

her lightly on the back of the neck as his orgasm rushed through his body, draining him of his strength. They both collapsed against the window.

Finally Hayden straightened, lifting her in his arms and carrying her down the hall to his bedroom. He'd just claimed her in front of the world—his world, Vegas—and she would be his for all time.

Shelby called her mom—something she hadn't done the last time she and Hayden had planned to marry. Her mother was so happy for her and was driving to Vegas to spend a few weeks with Shelby. Next she called Paige, who promised to fly back for the wedding.

Shelby flew to D.C. for her meetings but missed Hayden horribly. More than she'd thought she would. They talked every night about everything and nothing. And for the first time in a long time, Shelby felt as if she was flying home, to her real home, when she returned to Vegas.

Hayden had suggested they exchange vows in the gazebo in the middle of the maze where they'd made love. She'd agreed.

Everything was going very smoothly—too smoothly. She knew she had to say something to Hayden before his father did. Alan was everywhere, always watching her with that gaze that said she wasn't good enough for his son. She knew it. He knew it. Only Hayden didn't seem to sense the undercurrents.

But she suspected he did. Suspected he was putting all of that down to the past. But Shelby knew that it was more.

And finally, after weeks of anticipation, tonight was her last chance to say something. Her last chance to come clean before the wedding tomorrow. It was the rehearsal dinner, being thrown at the Golden Dream by Deacon and Kylie.

Earlier today Hayden had taken her riding on his Harley out in the desert. She'd planned to tell him then but had chickened out. The day had been perfect, a quiet sharing of their thoughts, the kind of experience that made her realize how much she loved him. How much she didn't want to hurt him.

Now they were back at the penthouse. Hayden was on the phone talking with his security people. They'd found the man who'd attacked Roxy, and Hayden's lawyers were making sure the man went to jail forever. Shelby was dressing—or trying to, at least. Nothing she put on looked right. She'd changed clothes fifteen times.

Finally she just stood in front of the full-length mirror and stared at herself in frustration. Tears burned the back of her eyes and she just couldn't take the internal pressure anymore. She had to say something.

"Baby? What's wrong?" Hayden asked as he crossed the room to her.

He wrapped his arms around her, pulling her back into the shelter of his body. As she stood there, surrounded by him, her fears seemed ridiculous. Surrounded by him she felt as if there was no way he'd ever let her go. Surrounded by him she felt like the lowest person alive. She never should have let this go on so long.

He tipped her head back and lowered his mouth to

hers. He never said he loved her. But in that kiss she felt his emotions. They flooded her and wrapped around her wounded heart, assuring her that everything would be okay.

"I thought you were going to wear that sexy red dress," he said when he lifted his head. He skimmed his hands down the curves of her body. "But I like this dress."

It was a black cocktail number with a plunging neckline. The dress had no back and was held up by a wide band of rhinestones at the neck. The skirt was full, ending just above her knees. She'd pulled her hair up and left a few tendrils curling at her neck and the sides of her face.

"The red one didn't look right," she said. "I'm not sure about this one, either. I want everything to be perfect tonight."

"It will be. Clothing doesn't matter."

"Not to you. You look perfect no matter what you wear."

And he did. Tonight he wore a custom-made tuxedo that he'd special ordered from his Savile Row tailor a few days ago. She was so outclassed and not just by the clothing.

"What are you afraid of?" he asked.

"Everything and everyone. When we walk into that party tonight, once again everyone will know that you picked someone beneath you."

"Shel, no one thinks that. I'm a gambler. Half of the moneyed people in Vegas won't talk to me. The others only talk to me when they're winning. I've been the target of more accusations than you can imagine."

She shook her head at him. "But you're still so…sophisticated. I can't help it, Hayden. I feel like I'm one step away from the trailer park. And that all those people can see it."

"Don't do this to yourself. Your life is a success that few find, regardless of where they started. I'm so proud of you, of what you've achieved."

She smiled up at him. "Thank you. But…there's something I have to tell you."

"You love me, right?"

She swallowed. "More than I thought I could love another person. It's so intense sometimes I have to pinch myself to make sure it's real."

"Don't do that, Shel. I'm here and I'm real."

She wrapped her arms around his, needing to take some of his strength and confidence with her before she told him the truth of their meeting again.

Taking a deep breath, she stepped away and put a few feet between them.

"There is something else I have to tell you."

He turned to face her. With his brooding eyes, she knew he sensed he wasn't going to like what she had to say. For a moment she considered never saying a word but she knew that Alan wouldn't let the truth lie undiscovered for much longer.

The doorbell rang. "Can this wait?" Hayden asked.

She nodded, happy for the reprieve. She watched him leave, already feeling the coldness in the room and in her heart.

Twelve

Hayden crossed the room, grateful for the distraction. Though he'd never admit it out loud, he'd been afraid that something would happen and his wedding to Shelby wouldn't go off without a hitch. Turned out his gut was right—again.

He cursed when he saw his dad standing on the threshold. "Not now, Dad. Really, I'm not in the mood for one of your lectures. And we have to get over to Deacon's."

His father wore a suit by the same tailor as Hayden's. The cuff links that his grandfather had given him shone at his wrists. He was flawlessly dressed from head to toe. Hayden remembered what Shelby had said about clothing and understood what she meant for the very first time.

He'd never really thought about all he took for granted but now he understood that maybe he should have. There were differences between himself and Shelby he couldn't ever really comprehend.

"I'm not here to lecture. I have to tell you something," Alan said, crossing to the bar and pouring himself a drink.

This wasn't good. His dad gestured with the bottle and Hayden nodded. He had a feeling he was going to need the alcohol.

"Not you, too. What is it—confession day?" he asked, taking the glass from his father.

His dad clinked the rims together before tipping his back and draining it. "Who else is confessing?"

"My soon-to-be wife," Hayden said, draining his glass. He dropped it on the bar and reached for the bottle, refilling both of their glasses.

His father stopped him with a hand on his wrist. He seemed almost relieved. "Ah, well then, maybe I'm too late."

"Too late for what?" Hayden asked, knowing that he wasn't going to like the answer. But he hadn't gotten to where he was in business by ignoring the cold harsh facts that life sometimes dealt his way.

"To tell you that I bribed her to get her back to Vegas and take up with you again."

Hayden swallowed. "What did you offer her?"

"That's where I screwed up, son. I told her she could have whatever she asked for."

"Dammit, Dad."

Alan shook his head.

Hayden set his glass down on the bar and crossed to the partially opened doorway of his bedroom. There was no need to ask Shelby if his father's words were true. She was standing there in the shadows, tears running down her face.

She had her arms wrapped around her waist and he knew she was hurting, but he didn't give a damn. How the hell had he allowed himself to be duped by her again? Why the hell wasn't he enough for her? When the hell was he going to learn that money, not love, motivated Shelby Anne Paxton?

"Come on out. Let's hear what you were going to say," he said to her, pushing the door open.

"Not in front of your father," she said, her eyes begging him for a reprieve. But he wasn't feeling generous right now.

"Why not? You seem to have been conspiring with him all this time."

She grabbed a tissue from the box on the dresser and wiped her nose. "There was no conspiracy. Please believe me."

Alan stood in the doorway saying nothing. Hayden wanted his dad to leave. The old man wasn't helping. Hayden knew there was more to what Shelby was telling him than what his father knew. He was angry and he knew that part of it was because of his dad.

"You came back here because of me, remember?" Alan said.

Shelby flinched but didn't look away from either of

them. "You're right, Alan. And you did promise me something if I came back here."

Shelby's voice shook when she spoke. A change came over her and Hayden hardly recognized her.

"I'd hoped this would help undo the mistakes I'd made when you were young," Alan said.

"Looks like you bet on the wrong woman again," Hayden said softly.

He saw her flinch and knew that his words had cut her deep. He felt an answering wound on his heart. Deep inside, where he'd felt safe hiding the fact that he loved this woman.

"I deserved that," she said. "But I'm fighting for our future, Hayden. I'm going to have to demand that you don't make any more remarks like that."

"You're in no position to demand anything," Alan said.

"Don't help, Dad. You've done enough."

Shelby looked away from him and straight at his father. "You said I could name my price."

Money. He'd known that was what she wanted. But a part of him couldn't believe it. This was the woman who wouldn't take any money from him at the blackjack table. The woman who'd fought to get where she was. He knew that his anger was clouding his judgment, that he was missing something really important here. But he couldn't put his finger on it.

He even understood why money was so important to her. But why couldn't she see that he had so much more to offer her? He could be her security if only she'd let him. "Dammit, Dad, you should have left this alone."

Alan stood in the corner, watching like the wily old gambler he was. Shelby watched him as if she wasn't sure whose side he was on. Hayden wanted to warn her the old man was always on his own side.

"What are you waiting for, Shelby?" Hayden stalked to his desk and pulled out his checkbook. "Name your price."

"I don't want a check."

"It's good."

"I'm sure it is. But the only thing I want is you, Hayden. I came back to Vegas for one reason—to reclaim the man I never forgot."

"My father bribed you."

"He threatened to go to the magazines with the truth about how I got the money to start the boutique. Tell them that Paige and I would do anything for money. I couldn't let him do that. But I sold myself once and I never will again. After he left my office, I realized that I'd never stopped thinking about you and…well, it seemed like the perfect chance to come back and take that gamble I wouldn't the first time."

Hayden dropped his pen and checkbook and she saw in his eyes the flame of desire and the hope for the future. "What gamble is that?"

"Double or nothing. Without you by my side that's what I have. Nothing."

"Looks like I won again," Alan said, finally bowing out gracefully, as if he suddenly accepted the inevitable. "Now get busy and give me some grandkids to spoil."

* * *

Hayden was staring at her as if he didn't recognize her. She closed the gap between them, taking his hand in hers. She lifted it to her face and kissed him gently. She knew she'd given him the shock of a lifetime and couldn't bear the thought of losing this man again.

"I appealed to the gambler in you because I know that you like to take long-shot bets. But if that doesn't work, then I'll beg. And if that doesn't work, then I'll simply stay here and wear you down until you can see the truth."

"What truth is that?" he asked, his voice low and husky.

"That I'm not asking you to take this leap by yourself. I'm scared of your world, of not fitting in. I'm scared to stay with a man who doesn't love me. But I'm more afraid of living the rest of my days in that lonely state that my life had become without you."

He said nothing and she couldn't stand the intensity in his eyes. She took a few steps away, reaching behind her to steady herself on the edge of the couch.

"You're wrong, Shel," he said, his voice deep and husky, brushing over her senses like a warm desert breeze.

"Wrong about what?" she asked. She was afraid that it was too late for them and she didn't want to give up hope. Not yet.

"Me not loving you."

"Really, Hayden, you don't have to say it. I know you can never love a woman whom you can't trust. You won't even have a wedding ceremony where you wait for me at the front of the chapel."

He closed the distance between them in three long strides. Grabbing her shoulders and pulling her up toward him, he took her mouth in a fierce kiss that left her battered soul wanting more.

"You're right, I didn't trust you. But I'vc loved you for more years than either of us realized. And my anger at you and my dad…well, it was due to the fact that I didn't have the courage to go and find you."

"You didn't know where I was."

"I never tried to look. I do love you, Shelby. I meant what I said when I asked you to marry me—you make all of this worthwhile."

Hayden pulled her down onto the couch, but the subsequent pounding on the door pulled them apart. "Go away. We're not available right now," he called out.

"Oh, hell, yes you are. I'm not going back to Kylie and telling her the guests of honor are no-shows."

Hayden cursed but she saw the smile in his eyes. He rubbed away the tracks her tears had made on her face and kissed her gently. "Later, I'm going to make love to you. But for now, let's go celebrate our marriage."

Hayden nervously stood in front of the preacher at the outdoor gazebo in the gardens at the Chimera. The afternoon was perfect, with the sun shining brightly down on them. Deacon stood at his side and Hayden was glad to have his friend there. Scott Rivers and Max Williams were there as well, serving as ushers. The two bachelors couldn't believe he'd given up his single days so easily. Hayden didn't even attempt to explain that life without Shelby wasn't nearly the ride that life with her was.

Shelby's mother waved at him from her seat in the front row, Roxy beside her. The two women had bonded. Terri Paxton needed to mother someone and Roxy needed someone to take care of her as her wounds healed, both mentally and physically. Terri was a stunningly beautiful woman and she loved Shelby. Shelby and Hayden were trying to convince Terri to move back to Vegas, and she was thinking it over.

His dad sat on the opposite side of the aisle, arms crossed over his chest, looking like a man who'd gotten what he wanted. Hayden shook his head thinking about how his father had played him and Shelby. But he couldn't be angry, not anymore. Hayden was grateful his father had interfered for once. Otherwise, he'd still be missing Shelby.

The music started and Hayden turned to wait for his bride. He'd been reluctant to do this again, to wait for her at the end of the aisle with his friends in attendance, but ultimately it was a little gesture that had meant a lot to Shelby and to their life together.

Paige came up the aisle first and then came Shelby. She came to him on her own, with no family to give her away. He felt the depth of his love for her overwhelm him, and tears burned the back of his eyes. Never had he guessed that she would mean this much to him.

She reached his side and he took her small trembling hand in his. Though the preacher was saying words of welcome to the congregation, Hayden bent and kissed Shelby.

She smiled up at him. His heart kicked and his gut tightened. Being married to Shelby was like winning the grand prize.

WHAT HAPPENS IN VEGAS…
is supposed to stay in Vegas.
But what happens when scandal leaks out?
Turn the page for a sneak preview of
the next provocative and sensual romance in
Katherine Garbera's juicy miniseries,
HER HIGH-STAKES AFFAIR -
March 2006
Available at your favorite retail outlet.

One

"**H**ey, sexy lady. Where do you want me today?"

Raine Montgomery bit the inside of her cheek and forced herself not to respond to Scott Rivers. Every morning it was the same line, or some variation of it. It should have sounded like a pick-up line but didn't. Instead, he made her want to believe she was a sexy lady—even though she'd had enough experience with gamblers to know they never told the truth.

"Can't decide?" he asked, slipping an arm around her waist.

She stepped away from him. "In your chair at the table."

"Honey, when are you going to loosen up with me?"

"When you stop flirting with every woman who walks by."

"Is it making you jealous?"

"No."

He laughed and walked away from her as the other players trickled in.

She'd gotten into the film business for one reason and one reason only—she'd dreamed of the day when she'd be called on the stage at the Academy Awards to accept her Oscars for best director and film of the year. She even had her speech rehearsed.

I'd like to thank the Academy for recognizing my accomplishments, and I'd like the rest of the world to know that Missy Talbot is a spoiled bitch and my dad isn't a loser.

Okay, so it was a little melodramatic, but she'd been in junior high at the time and it had seemed like the perfect solution to her dismal and dreary life in Atlantic City, New Jersey.

But her dream hadn't gotten her to the Oscar's. In fact, she wasn't even close to winning a People's Choice award, or any award at all. She doubted anyone was going to be giving her recognition for directing Celebrity Poker Challenge.

The show ran for four weeks. They had three celebrities and three champions from across the country to compete. In each week's episode, two games were played and at the end of the show two players were eliminated. At the end, the remaining two players played two high-stakes games to determine the Celebrity Poker Champ.

Each person on the show signed a waiver promising not to reveal the results of the show. Viewers had the chance to vote on who they thought was the best and win a myriad of prizes that had been donated by sponsors. The celebrities were playing for charities as were the champions.

She'd given all the players wide berth because her producer, Joel Tanner, didn't like her or any of the crew fraternizing with them. In fact, there was a clear no-fraternization clause in the contracts everyone on the set signed for both in front of the camera and behind the scenes. He wanted to make sure they didn't end up with a lawsuit because of the way the players were shown.

She rubbed the back of her neck and headed toward the director's booth. Some people called it the God booth because she wasn't on the set and her voice could be heard but she couldn't be seen. But Raine knew she was as far from God as any person could be.

Especially right now, since she was having impure thoughts about Scott. She entered the booth and put on her headphones. All of the players were miked and she heard their small talk.

The deep, sexy tones of Scott's voice came over her headphones and she paused to listen.

"Shot down again, eh, stud?"

Scott glanced over at Stevie Taylor, the notoriously debauched lead singer for the heavy metal rock band Viper, which had been on the cutting edge of music fifteen years ago. Stevie had the kind of talent and energy that had kept him in the mainstream, changing his style through the years to fit the younger audiences' tastes.

That being said, the man was an ass sometimes and Scott suspected Stevie was still pissed about losing to him at the PGA/Celebrity golf tournament last month in Hawaii. Or maybe it was the fact that Scott had unwittingly been the object of Stevie's third wife's affection.

"Some women take more time than others," Scott said. "They aren't all impressed with long hair and fast cars."

"I guess that means you have to try harder?" Stevie said.

There was an edge to his voice that Scott chose to ignore. Every day was work for Scott. He'd grown up on a soundstage and had learned early on to act the way others found acceptable. With Stevie, he acted like a babe magnet, always on the prowl because that was what the legendary rock front-man understood. With Raine he acted…unfortunately he wasn't doing such a great job of it. She made him forget he was playing a role.

"Sure. Everything worth having takes some effort." And Raine was definitely worth the effort. He wondered how she felt about the no-fraternization clause they'd both signed. Scott was honest enough to admit that the gambler in him wanted to take a chance on her.

"You're working up a sweat and she's barely noticing you, Rivers. What would your fan club say?"

Scott didn't respond to the goad. He didn't have a fan club and Stevie knew it. His child stardom had translated into cult-classic films in his early twenties and two one-offs that had turned into blockbusters. He acted when he felt like it, preferring to spend most of his time working with the charitable trust he set up with his own money. "I'm not worried, Stevie."

"Some boys aren't meant to play in the big leagues," the other man said.

"Whatever. You know she can't really show that she's attracted to me."

"Because she isn't?" Stevie said with a snicker.

"Because we work together." A man like Stevie would never understand the distinction, but Scott knew that Raine would. That her job and her reputation would be important to her. He understood why.

"I wouldn't let that stop me."

He wasn't going to do this. Defend himself like some sort of teenage boy with his first woman. Scott was thirty-eight, long grown up; he wouldn't get drawn into this conversation.

"What, no glib remark?"

Stevie wasn't going to let this go. Scott had to find a way to shut him up.

"What would it take for you to drop this?"

"How about a little wager?"

"On a woman? Have you been living under a rock for the last twenty years?"

"There's no reason anyone other than the two of us has to know about it."

Famous last words. He glanced around the set. They were far enough away from anyone that they had the kind of privacy that was something of a luxury on a television or movie set.

"What'd you have in mind?"

"A simple bet…you get her in bed before the show wraps."

Scott felt a tingling at the back of his neck that he always got before he did something risky. Like sky surfing or kayaking down a class VI rapid. Something that all of his self-preservation instincts said not to do. But if it got Stevie off his back, then it might be worth it.

"You're on. What's the wager?"

"Fifty thousand."

"Okay."

THE
ELLIOTTS

Mixing business with pleasure

The series continues with

Cause for Scandal

by
ANNA DEPALO

(Silhouette Desire #1711)

She posed as her identical twin to meet a sexy
rock star—but Summer Elliott certainly didn't
expect to end up in bed with him. Now the
scandal is about to hit the news and she has
some explaining to do...to her prominent
family and her lover.

On sale March 2006!

Silhouette®
Desire.

Coming this March from

MARY LYNN BAXTER

Totally Texan

(Silhouette Desire #1713)

She's only in town for a few weeks…
certainly not enough time to start an
affair. But then she meets one totally
hot Texan male and all bets are off!

On sale March 2006!

HARLEQUIN *Presents*

We're delighted to announce that

A Mediterranean Marriage

is taking place—and you are invited!

Imagine blue skies, an azure sea, a beautiful landscape
and the hot sun. What a perfect place to get married!
But although all ends well for these couples, their
route to happiness is filled with emotion and passion.

Follow their journey in the latest book
from this miniseries.

In **THE GREEK'S CHOSEN WIFE,**
Prudence Demarkis will consummate her
marriage to tycoon Nikolos Angelis. She wants
a baby, he wants a wife; together they will
learn to make a marriage.

Get your copy today!

**THE GREEK'S CHOSEN WIFE is on sale
March 2006, wherever books are sold.**

If you enjoyed what you just read,
then we've got an offer you can't resist!

Take 2 bestselling
love stories FREE!
Plus get a FREE surprise gift!

From reader-favorite

Kathie DeNosky

THE ILLEGITIMATE HEIRS

A brand-new miniseries about three brothers denied a father's name, but granted a special inheritance.

Don't miss:

Engagement between Enemies

(Silhouette Desire #1700, on sale January 2006)

Reunion of Revenge

(Silhouette Desire #1707, on sale February 2006)

Betrothed for the Baby

(Silhouette Desire #1712, on sale March 2006)

COMING NEXT MONTH

#1711 CAUSE FOR SCANDAL—Anna DePalo
The Elliotts
She posed as her identical twin and bedded a rock star—now the shocking truth is about to be revealed!

#1712 BETROTHED FOR THE BABY—Kathie DeNosky
The Illegitimate Heirs
What happens when coworkers playing husband and wife begin wishing they were betrothed for real?

#1713 TOTALLY TEXAN—Mary Lynn Baxter
He's the total Texan package and she's just looking for a little rest and relaxation…. Sounds perfect—until their hearts get involved.

#1714 HER HIGH-STAKES AFFAIR—Katherine Garbera
What Happens in Vegas…
An affair between them is forbidden, but all bets are off when passion strikes under the neon lights of Vegas!

#1715 A SPLENDID OBSESSION—Cathleen Galitz
She was back in town to get her life together…not fall for a man who dared her to be his inspiration.

#1716 SECRETS IN THE MARRIAGE BED—Nalini Singh
Will an unplanned pregnancy save a severed marriage and rekindle a love that's been stifled for five years?

SDCNM0206